GILDAEN

GILDAEN

THE HEROIC ADVENTURES
OF A MOST UNUSUAL RABBIT

Emilie Buchwald

Illustrated by Barbara Flynn

HARCOURT BRACE JOVANOVICH, INC.
NEW YORK

To my father,
the best storyteller I know,
and to my children,
the best story-listeners

CONTENTS

GILDAEN

ILDAEN WAS THAT RARITY AMONG RABBITS, AN adventurer. He had always been more curious, more daring than his brothers and sisters, though he resembled them in every other particular. While they were playing games together, he liked to creep away from the watchful eye of his mother to explore. Not far from his burrow and thicket in the Lower Wood was a castle on the brow of a low hill. No one lived in it anymore. The outer towers were crumbling into ruin, the windows were dark, and the moat was empty and had become a home for toads who enjoyed the mud. The walls were covered with a

7

thick overgrowth of ivy, prying into the crannies and crevices of the stone.

In the courtyard the castle garden lived on, grown wild and thick with a tangle of weeds and grasses. Tall stalks of darnel and stinging nettle flourished in once well-tended flower beds. Pliant tendrils of sweet woodbine twined greedily about the old trees. Gildaen ventured there whenever he had the chance. Of course he had been warned— more than once!—never to go there, for it was a deserted spot, a good hiding place for outlaw creatures. A more sensible rabbit, or an older and more experienced one, would have been properly afraid to cross the splintered drawbridge, leaving the protection of tall grasses and thickets, but no thought of possible danger troubled Gildaen.

He liked to browse among the old garden beds, sampling and savoring the unfamiliar plants. After one unfortunate experience with a swarm of bees, he stayed away from the wild thyme which the bees visited much of the summer day. The herb garden was especially interesting to him, for the tastes were unusual and pleasing. There were plants in the garden that he had never seen elsewhere. The lettuce he thought of as mild-crunch, and the spinach leaves as tasty-tart. He ate the poppies with their tangy seeds despite the fact that they generally gave him a stomachache. Gildaen did pretty much as he wanted to do, no matter what the outcome.

One afternoon in the fall of the year, while he was lying almost asleep in the weeds, he heard a dreaded sound. The fur on his back stood up, while his ears sank down trembling.

The sound was soft, throaty, mournful, a sound he had heard at night; it was frightening even when he was safely nestled in his burrow deep within the thicket, a sound that floated down to him like a dark feather.

"No!" he thought. "Not in the daytime. No! It can't be an owl!"

But it was. Whizzing over his head came the winged gray shape. It grazed the tops of his down-folded ears. At any moment Gildaen expected to be borne up and up in the unyielding grip of the owl's talons, to feel them in his fur, biting into his sides, to be taken away as he had seen one of his brothers swooped up, never to return. But nothing of the sort happened.

He opened his eyes, then shut them again. Directly before him stood the owl, who was glaring at him with a terrible, fierce look in his yellow eyes.

"Who am I?" asked the owl, in a voice that Gildaen thought surprisingly gentle. The rabbit opened his eyes again, but dared not to speak, and so the owl asked the same question again, this time a bit impatiently. But still Gildaen could not bring himself to answer. He was far too frightened.

"Well, well, why don't you speak, you furry little nothing!" The owl hopped one step closer to the place where Gildaen was cowering.

"Oh, sir, you are an owl—a very large owl!" he whimpered.

"Hmm," said the bird. Then he seemed to forget about the rabbit, who was seeking to make himself as small and insignificant-looking as possible. Every now and again the owl ruffled his feathers as he stood lost in thought. The minutes passed with a dreadful slowness. Gildaen felt as if he could scarcely breathe. At last the owl peered at him again, examining him with close attention.

"If, as you tell me, I am an owl, I can understand why

the light seems far too bright to suit my taste. If, as you say, I am an owl, I suppose I ought to make a dinner out of you."

Every bit of Gildaen shook at these words.

"No, no! Stop that quivering! I wouldn't think of eating you, you ridiculous bit of fluff. Remember that I said 'if' to all this. Let me just make certain for myself."

The owl hopped to the courtyard fountain, partly filled with brackish rainwater, and perching on the rim, gazed down at his reflection. Gildaen was trying to decide whether he should take this chance and run, run as he never had before in his short life. He could imagine himself leaping into the air in great bounds, if only he could get started, but his feet seemed frozen to the ground. He promised himself that if he could manage to escape, he would never again tease his sisters, or trick his brothers into landing in mud puddles, or come to this frightful place, ever, ever again.

But it was too late. The owl hopped back.

"You are correct, young sir. I am indeed an owl. For the present. Do you understand?" He said this in a friendly, conversational tone.

Gildaen swallowed and managed to say squeakily, "No, my lord owl."

The owl whispered the word: "Enchantment!"

Gildaen only looked as puzzled as he felt.

The owl spoke louder: "Magic! Spells! Enchantment! Bewitchment of some kind! Now do you understand?"

"Do you mean, sir," asked the rabbit timidly, "that you are not an owl?"

"Exactly!" the owl fairly shouted, hopping up and down in his excitement. "You do have some brain after all! No, I am not an owl—that is, I am not *really* an owl!"

"But, then, what are you?" Gildaen inquired.

"A good query. But not the most important question as far as I can see. You ought better to ask—*who* am I?"

Gildaen was beginning to take some little pleasure in this conversation. "Very well," he asked. "Who are you?"

The owl was once more lost in thought. He mumbled, half aloud, "Who am I, who am I?" He glared at Gildaen. "*Whooo* am I? Who *am* I? Who am *I?* There it is in a nutshell. I do not know. Haven't any idea at all. Any more than you have."

Gildaen was silent since the owl seemed so irritated and upset.

"I thought at first that I must be an enchanted prince, but that is not right, I am sure." And, to illustrate these words, the owl began to change his shape and grow before Gildaen's eyes, until in place of the owl there stood a tall boy with scarlet hose and a jeweled cloak. He wore a circlet of gold around his brow. On his right hand a great ring of gold, set with an enormous ruby, gleamed with crimson fire in the sunshine.

"You see?" the boy prince said conversationally to the rabbit, as if nothing uncommon had just taken place. "I have already thought of the obvious. The natural course of events, it seemed to me, was that a sorcerer had turned me from a prince to something else, so I tried to turn myself back. It was quite easy. I thought what a prince should look like, and before I knew it, there I was, as you see me now. But when I looked down at myself, I knew that I had not started out as a prince. I knew, too, that I had some errand to perform, an important one I am sure, but so deep a cloud is on my memory that I can remember nothing further back than yesterday morning." The boy prince sat down near Gildaen despondently.

"You can remember nothing?" Gildaen inquired, interested and greatly relieved now that he was no longer dealing with an owl.

"Nothing! I thought of one creature after another, and I found that by concentrating on any one of them, I could assume its form."

"You mean that you can be anyone or anything you wish?" Gildaen asked, his excitement growing.

"So it would seem." The boy prince picked a blade of grass and chewed on it reflectively. "But I want more than anything else to be me, if only I can discover who 'me' is. For the present, I may as well continue in this shape."

"But," Gildaen insisted, "don't you know where you've come from? I mean, before you flew here?"

"I only remember finding myself in a garden, much better tended than this one. No one came when I called out. I was confused and very sleepy, as if I had awakened from a long night's dreaming wearing someone else's nightclothes. I spent that whole day thinking myself into different forms, and I must have dozed off once more. When I awoke, the sun was rising. It seemed to me that it would be a pleasant experience to be able to fly. Next thing I knew, there I was, up in the air, winging away from that place, flying south. I have been flying all day, until now when I spied you down here, imagining yourself well hidden, I don't doubt!"

Gildaen hung his head, feeling most foolish. He had thought himself completely safe in his hiding place.

"As it happens, I was curious and not the least bit hungry when I dropped down to look you over. Although, now that I think of it, I find that I have become dreadfully hungry."

"Wouldn't you care for some of these greens, your high-

ness?" asked Gildaen, nodding toward the beds of vegetables growing wild.

The prince shook his head. "I think not. I won't be *that*
hungry for a while, my friend, but thank you just the
same."

Gildaen had been noticing that the manners of the
prince were a good deal better than those of the owl. He
looked carefully around the garden courtyard, trying to
imagine what might suit a prince's appetite. His attention
was drawn to the old trellises near the south wall, still
laden with a few bunches of dark grapes.

"Would your highness care for the purple berries that
grow over there?" he inquired, moving toward the old
grape arbor.

"The very thing, rabbit, the very thing!" replied the
prince with enthusiasm, following Gildaen. He reached
up and gathered the grapes that the birds had not already
eaten. They sat in the grass together, the prince stripping
the vine, while Gildaen waited for his share. Gildaen
thought he had never tasted anything more delicious. But
there were very few grapes. His first fear had completely
disappeared, and he was thoroughly enjoying himself. The
boy prince was smiling at him.

"You are cleverer than you first appeared, rabbit. Do
you know the name of these fruits?"

"No, your highness."

"These grapes, as they are called, are excellent just as
they are from the vine, but when their juices are pressed
and aged, they become a drink called wine, which is both
delicious and helpful in treating some kinds of sickness."

Gildaen said excitedly, "Perhaps you could make more
of them!"

"Make more of them?" said the boy. "What do you mean?"

"Well," said Gildaen boldly, "you can change yourself into anything. Why could you not change these empty vines into full ones?"

"An intelligent thought," answered the prince. "I will try."

Gildaen sat expectantly as the boy prince gazed intently at the vines. Several minutes passed by and nothing happened. The boy frowned and shook his head. "Sorry, my friend," he said. "I cannot oblige you. Although I can change myself, I do not seem to be able to get us more grapes."

"Never mind, your highness," said Gildaen. "Perhaps you used to tend these fruits, and that is why you know their names and what use they have?"

"I'm not sure," answered the prince, licking his sticky fingers. "It seems to me that I know the names of all the herbs and plants growing here and that I understand their powers."

"I have always wanted to know their real names," ventured Gildaen hesitantly. "Would you teach them to me?"

The boy prince shook his head. "I cannot be your teacher now; first I must find out who I am, even though I am not sure where or how to begin."

Gildaen was disappointed. At last he had met someone who was able to tell him what he longed to know but who would soon leave here forever. Then this adventure would end, and he would go back to his burrow no wiser than before. An idea came to him, an idea so unlikely that he wondered how he had ever dared to think it.

"Your highness," he said softly, plucking up his courage, "may I come with you?"

The prince looked down at him, obviously much surprised at his request.

"You? But why? Why should you wish to join me? I do
not know myself where I am going. I shall have to wander
about. There will be discomfort, perhaps lack of food, and
certainly, for a rabbit, there will be danger. You might
never see your home again."

"But, sir," Gildaen said, "I have always wanted to see
more of the world. Often I have lain here and dreamed of
the wide lands that stretch farther than I can see from the
highest hill. I wonder what life is like in other places.
Maybe it is dangerous to go. Maybe, as my mother says, I
will come to a sorry end, on the spit or in the stewpot. But
I want to go with you nonetheless." He added, shyly, "I
want to learn the names of the plants."

"Strange," said the prince with a laugh. "Who would
have thought that a wanderer's heart lay in the breast of
a rabbit!" He yawned and held out his arms, stretching
them over his head. "Let us take some rest together here
in the sun's last warmth, and then, my friend, we will
decide."

He took off his shining cloak and spread it on the turf.
"Ah," he said with a sigh as he lay down on his back,
hands propped beneath his head, "flying is a tiring activity,
I find." Soon he was breathing regularly, lost in sleep.

Gildaen thought that he looked most regal as he lay
there. "How can I come to harm," he thought, "with such
a protector?"

That autumn afternoon, with leaves their most brilliant
shades of orange and gold, the world seemed an inviting
place. "Yes, surely," he thought, "it is right and proper,
when one is young and keen, to travel and to learn." He
felt himself grow sleepy in the warm sun.

A NIGHT IN THE CASTLE

 ILDAEN AWOKE SUDDENLY, AND IN CONFUSION, to find the afternoon almost gone. He was startled to think that he had slept so long out in the open. Then he remembered the prince at whose side he had dozed off and whose presence had given him a new feeling of safety.

But the prince was nowhere to be seen. Had he only dreamed the meeting with the owl? He examined the grasses; the imprint of the cloak was clearly visible. The encounter had been real! Where, he wondered, was the prince?

16

"He's gone off and left me," he said, half aloud, "because he thought I would be a burden to him." It was hard to accept the fact that his adventure was over. Bad end or not, he felt that he would never be happy if he was forced to spend all his days in sight of the place of his birth.

Gildaen leaped onto a stone bench beside the grape arbor and listened, his ears attentive to every sound. He heard, or thought he heard, the murmur of voices and, from somewhere not far away, a muffled laugh. Then there was silence. Ordinarily, these noises would have alarmed and alerted him, but today he was too concerned with finding the prince to pay heed. In the orchard beyond the crumbled east wall of the castle, he caught a glimpse of red and gold. The sun's westering rays shone on the prince's ruby ring as he raised his hand in greeting to Gildaen.

"Here I am!" he called. He returned at a brisk pace through a breach in the wall.

"I've found some apples!" he said, and emptying his cloak in the grass, he joined Gildaen on the bench.

"Your highness!" Gildaen said, overcome with joy to find the prince again. "I thought you had left me!"

"Left?" The prince frowned. "You mean without saying farewell? I would hardly do that, my friend, though perhaps that would be the kindest thing I could do for you. When I awoke, you were sound asleep. I found stramony —you call it thorn apple—in the herb garden, and I took a piece of its root. It is precious indeed, for even a small bit crushed and mixed with water will give the gift of sleep without pain." He crunched into an apple. "Delicious! By the way, have you a name?"

"I am called Gildaen, sir."

"And you say you would like to accompany me, Gildaen?"

"I should like to follow you, sir, and to learn from you, especially the lore of plants." Then he added, his eyes modestly turned to the apples, "It may be that I can be of some help to you."

The prince stared at him intently as he finished one apple and chose a second. "Perhaps. But you would be of more help to me if you could better understand what is going on around you. For instance, have you ever before been able to speak with a boy or—for that matter—with an owl?"

"Oh, no!" Gildaen replied.

"And yet you have not wondered how it is that you and I could talk with one another?"

"I suppose I was too frightened to think about it at first," Gildaen said, "and then I got used to it."

"Have an apple, Gildaen," urged the prince. "You see, I find myself able to understand the tongue of every creature and to speak to every creature in its own proper speech. As we sit here, I hear the birds chattering of foul weather soon to come."

"I can only hear them whistling and chirruping, as usual."

"And I suppose you don't hear the field mice preparing winter quarters by the wall over there?"

"Yes, I hear them, and I can catch a few words of their talk, though it's not familiar to me, by any means. But I can understand the speech of almost all the folk, the small folk, who live in the Lower Wood."

"To be my companion, Gildaen, you will need to understand more. I wonder if I can help you. Let me try. Look at me!" he commanded. Gildaen looked.

Those steady eyes stared into his, and they seemed to

search his very being, seeing what he was and what he knew. He heard a voice, and yet the prince had not spoken. The voice seemed to be speaking within himself. It was saying, "Listen, Gildaen, listen as you never have before!"

His ears quivered. He had always thought himself a good listener. He prided himself on his ability to hear the snap of the smallest twig on the forest floor beneath the wary feet of the fox. Now, in an instant, to his amazement and delight, the bird calls turned into conversations. A mother wren was telling her cocky young ones about the flight south they would soon make. "There's bad weather coming!" she squawked.

"I can understand them! I know what they're saying!" Gildaen burst out excitedly.

"Good," said the prince. "I was able to help you. You can speak now to every living being that creeps, walks, swims, or flies, and you will understand their replies. Use your knowledge wisely!"

"I promise, sir, I shall!"

"Remember, this knowledge will lead you into the possession of secrets you would never know otherwise. You must think twice before you reveal a word, for you may betray the weak and helpless into the jaws of their enemies!"

The boy's face was stern and forbidding as he spoke. Gildaen felt once more the hidden power of his new friend.

"I am young, I know, but I will keep every secret as if it were my own life I defended," said Gildaen.

"Well spoken!" said the prince. He selected a few of the apples and stood up. "Now we need a place to lay our heads tonight."

"One moment, please, sir. What name am I to call you?"

"Name? Why, as I have none at the present, you must give me one, until I find my own again."

Gildaen said shyly, "Would 'Evon' do? That's my eldest brother's name. I could call you Prince Evon."

"Splendid! Keep calling me 'Evon' until I remember that you are talking to *me*," he said.

They both turned to the castle behind them. The light from the setting sun touched its cold grayness with a momentary glow of orange-gold light. Then, as the light began to fail, the castle looked to Gildaen more and more like a gigantic dark animal hunched and waiting.

"Why should we not find shelter there, Gildaen?" mused the prince.

Gildaen was terrified of the castle, especially now in the twilight. The prince walked confidently toward the tower door, but Gildaen's heart was pounding so fast that he was unable to move a step.

His instincts warned him that the place was dangerous, yet he hesitated to confess his fear to the prince. How could he go adventuring in the wide world if he could not even face entering this castle so close to his own home?

The massive door on its hinges of rusty iron stood slightly ajar. Gildaen thought it strange that the door should be open at all. The prince pulled it open still farther with his free hand, holding onto the apples with the other. As he crossed the stone threshold, an arm seized him and covered his mouth, while another closed around his throat, drawing him backward and spilling the apples. Immediately a crowd of men came forward from the shadows, laughing at the sight of the captive.

Gildaen remembered the laugh and the murmur of voices he had heard earlier. "I am a fool!" he thought. "And I have allowed him to be trapped."

One fellow whose crafty face peered from beneath a

dark hood called out, "Here, Hickory, bring him into the hall, so's we can have a look at him by the fire."

When Gildaen witnessed the capture of the prince, he had leaped back into the shadow of the door. Now, forcing himself forward, he followed the men, staying always in the darkest part of the passage. Only concern for the prince's safety could have made him step inside that fearful passageway. The men went into the great hall, arguing and talking over the prisoner. Gildaen stuck his head around the corner so that he might watch.

No one was looking in his direction. They were all intent on Evon, who was standing before the stone hearth in which a puny fire had been kindled. Behind him, no longer holding his arms, was the largest man in the room. He was not in the least bit fat, though at first Gildaen had thought him so, before he saw that his great arms and legs were all muscle. He had a neck like the trunk of a sturdy young tree. His blue eyes were set in a broad face topped by a thatch of almost white hair that looked as soft and fine as a baby's as it spilled onto his forehead.

"That is not an unkind face," thought Gildaen.

Around the prince in a half-circle, the other men stood or sprawled. Gildaen counted more than a dozen before the strain of counting so high made him stop. They were a rough-looking lot, ill cared for, with patched clothes and dirty faces and, worst of all, expressions that betokened no good to the prisoner. Gildaen wondered if Evon was afraid. The boy was looking steadily about him, examining his captors as if they, and not he, were the prisoners. The firelight shone on the jewels embroidered in his cloak. His ring sent out ruddy fires of its own as he moved his hand.

The hooded man faced him, pointing a finger. "Here, you, stop giving us the eye!"

"What do you mean?" answered Evon calmly.

"I mean you've no right to act so high and mighty with us, you young jackanapes!"

"Why did you seize me?" Evon asked calmly.

"I said, never mind that high-born manner; just don't you forget who's in charge!"

"Don't you have a name?" Evon asked, unruffled by the man's fierce annoyance.

"Chough is the name, and I want to know right quick who *you* are! I'll ask the questions from now on."

The prince said nothing; he gazed into the fire thoughtfully as if he were in the hall alone. Gildaen admired him very much, but he was afraid of the man called Chough.

"So you won't give us an answer, eh? Well, never fear, we'll make you glad enough to talk before we're finished with you!"

"Let's have his cloak!" called one of the men.

"Take his ring!" shouted another who had been gazing at it greedily.

"Slip a knife between his ribs and throw him in the dungeons to rot, Chough! Not a soul will see him again," said a third.

"Burn his fingers—that'll make him talk!"

The men jumped up and crowded threateningly about the boy.

"No!" said a deep, slow voice. The man called Hickory stepped forward and placed his hands on the boy's shoulders. "No one will hurt him. The first man who touches him I will break in two."

His words were calm and deliberate, but his mild blue eyes had a dangerous gleam. The men drew back, muttering and complaining.

"What cowards they really are," thought Gildaen. He was grateful to the big man, for he saw that the others held him in healthy respect, and he knew that things might have gone ill for Evon if he had not intervened.

"Thank you, my friend," said the prince, without turning.

"I do not know if I am your friend, boy, but I will not let you be hurt. Only wicked and weak men would do those things they spoke of." He looked directly at Chough, who turned his eyes away.

"Now, take it easy, Hickory. We was just tryin' to fright the lad into tellin' us what he's doin' here. Don't forget it was him who walked into our hideout."

Hickory nodded. "That is true. Boy, why have you come here?"

"I am called Evon, and to you I will tell what there is to tell. I am lost, tired, hungry, and homeless. I needed a place to sleep and thought to find it here."

The others jeered and hooted, making rude noises and catcalls at this answer.

"He's hungry! With those geegaws on him!"

"Look at 'is clothes. 'E's never wanted for nothing! What a liar!"

"These?" asked the prince disdainfully, looking down at his clothes. "I do not want them. I will trade with any of you!" He unhooked his cloak and tossed it to one of the men. "Give me your ragged one in return," he said, and the man hastily handed over his own, clutching at the jeweled one.

"Me fortune's made," he said wonderingly.

"Take this, too, since you like it so well," said Evon, and he threw his ring into the air.

There was a general scramble on the floor for possession of the ring, until one man thrust it on his finger and stood ready to defend it with his dagger.

"He's a loony, Chough," said the man who had caught

the cloak. "He don't know the value of nothing—that's for sure."

"What about that gold circlet on yer forehead?" Chough asked roughly.

"You may have it, if you wish," said Evon, taking it from his brow.

Chough held the golden coronet admiringly and put it on his own head.

"Ouch! Blast the thing—it's too small and pinches!" He quickly took it off again. "But it's mine, just the same, do you hear?" he snarled, giving the others a suspicious glare. Then, for the first time, he smiled at Evon, a crooked mockery of a smile, as if his mouth were unaccustomed to this act.

"All right, lad. I guess we think better of yer company now. Mad as a dog you may be to give away yer finery, but I'll put a watch on you. Hickory, take the prisoner Evon to that corner there. See that he gets some grub and some straw to sleep on, but watch him close!"

Gildaen saw his friend led away from the fire to a bed of straw. The man Hickory brought him cold meat and dark bread and watched him as he ate.

The others had gathered still closer to the fire and appeared to be arguing. Gildaen listened with more curiosity than fear.

"No, Chough, I says it's a waste o' time. What's a farm widow got worth stealin'? I says let's rob the farmer we saw today. I'll warrant he's got what's worth takin'!"

"Yer wrong, mate," said Chough soothingly. "I've heard the talk in the village. They're a superstitious lot, but in this I'll wager there's truth. That widow's husband left her rich, but she's a miser and won't spend none of her gold, livin' in that tumbledown cottage and pretendin' she's poor. We'll make her tell us where the gold is hid. She's got a daughter, too, that she won't want to see hurt. By tomorrer night we'll be sittin' here sharin' out the gold!"

"Right you are, Chough; we'll have it!"

They sat around joking and passing a wineskin. After what seemed to Gildaen to be hours of drunken laughter and foolish, ugly talk, they stretched out where they were and slept.

CROWS

HE FIRE HAD BURNED DOWN LOW. THE COALS were barely glowing when Gildaen plucked up the courage to creep stealthily into the hall. He had to pick his way around the bodies of the sleeping men. One of them turned and flung his hand out. Gildaen had just enough time to jump away before the heavy hand landed where he had crouched a moment before. The sleepers snored and mumbled. Every instant Gildaen felt sure one of them would open his eyes and seize him. With a last leap across the sleeping form of Hickory, he landed beside the prince, who was lying on his heap of straw in the darkest corner of the hall. Evon immediately opened his eyes.

"I've been pretending to sleep for a long while," he whispered, "but I've been watching you, Gildaen. It was brave of you not to desert me."

"We must escape," urged Gildaen, whispering back. "Let's go while these wicked men are asleep!"

"Gildaen, the matter is not so simple. If you think about it for a minute, you will realize that I could have escaped at any time I desired to by changing myself into another shape."

"Then do so, Evon, sir! I think I will die of fright if we stay here much longer."

"You are already braver than when we met, Gildaen, so pay attention to what I say. Did you hear those men talking of the morrow?"

"Yes. They made some horrible plan or other. I didn't listen to the details too carefully."

"They intend to rob some poor woman and her daughter, and they have threatened to harm them unless they get the gold they are seeking. How can we run away and let them do these things?"

"But how can we prevent them? I can do nothing, and there are so many of them bigger and stronger than you. They will do anything to get what they want."

Evon's mouth was set in a firm line. "I do not know yet what we will do, but I am starting to make a plan. There is one trick that may work, if I can accomplish it."

Hickory stirred in his sleep. For a terrible instant it seemed to Gildaen that he would turn his head and look at them. Then he mumbled something that sounded like "No, my lord!", sighed deeply, and fell back into silence.

Gildaen's heart slowed a little. The prince motioned to the pile of dirty straw on which he lay.

"Creep in here, Gildaen. I'll make room for you and cover you over. No one will find you, and you will be able to stay near me."

Obediently Gildaen allowed himself to be covered over with straw. There was plenty of room for him, and the straw kept out some of the chill, although it tickled his fur and made his nose itch.

"Try to sleep, Gildaen. We must be alert in the morning."

Gildaen thought that he would never be able to rest in such a place, yet when he opened his eyes next, there was a faint gray light in the room and the robbers were building up the fire again, making preparations for a morning meal.

"You," sneered Chough, "you lazy slug-a-bed, get over there and stir the pot." He was standing over the prince. He gave him a kick with one booted foot. "Be quick about it, too!"

Evon stood up, rubbed his cold hands together, and took the wooden stirring spoon.

Hickory was tossing handfuls of dried oats into the kettle of boiling water.

"Stir, lad," he cautioned the prince. "Keep it well stirred, or there'll be lumps in the porridge."

Concealed in the straw, Gildaen watched the preparations unhappily. The men were taking turns sharpening their knives against a whetstone. Two of them were practicing their skill fighting with their cudgels until one caught the other off guard and give him a blow in the ribs that sent him to the floor screaming and cursing. The others laughed as he lay rolling on the floor in pain.

Evon dropped his spoon and ran to the fallen man. He pulled up the man's greasy jerkin.

"Tear me some strips of cloth, one of you!" he commanded. For a moment no one moved. Then Hickory strode over and tore the shirt off the back of the man who had cudgeled his opponent. Before the man could protest, he took away his cudgel, as easily as if the man had given it to him. He threw it into the hottest part of the fire.

"Here's your cloth, lad."

"Good. Now rip it into strips."

The man whose shirt it was reached out for it, but Hickory threw him a glance, and he drew back as Hickory quickly ripped up the shirt. The boy wound the strips of cloth around the man's bruised side.

"You've at least one broken rib," Evon told him gravely, "but if you keep as quiet as you can and leave on these wrappings, you will soon begin to mend."

The man continued his groaning. "You've hurt me worse," he cried. "I can't stand to have it bound so tight!" And he began to claw at the bandage.

"You are a fool!" said Hickory. "You do not know enough to thank one who would help you. Leave those strips alone! I have seen the king's physician do the same for men whose ribs were broken in battle. This boy Evon has skill."

The kettle began to steam furiously; the porridge bubbled over and hissed onto the fire below. Clouds of steam and the smell of burned porridge rose into the chamber.

"You're both to blame! Hickory, you blockhead, and this boy who fancies he's a great healer, you can't even cook porridge without burning it and scalding the rest of us!" yelled Chough, red in the face.

Hickory lifted the heavy kettle off the hook as if it were

a small pot. He did not try to defend himself from Chough's anger.

"And you two ninnies," Chough raged at the men who had been fighting, "what do you mean by knocking each other about when we've work to do? Get up, you, and leave the wrappings alone, I say. Get up, or you'll have no share of the gold."

The man on the floor pulled himself up, still muttering and groaning. Evon passed out the bowls of steaming porridge as Hickory ladled them. The injured man looked sourly at the boy and slumped down again on the straw.

"Eat up!" growled Chough. "And listen to what I've got to tell you. We're goin' to call on the Widow Flann. She lives a quick hour's walk east of us. We should get there well afore noon, provided we can get movin'." And he threw a look of disgust at the bandaged robber. "I'll go in first, pretendin' I'm on my way to the village lookin' for work, and I'll ask to rest my feet. That'll get me into the house so's I can have a look. If I find the gold, all's well. If not, then I'll let the widow know we mean to have it, one way or another. While I'm inside, you, mates, sneak through the fields and surround the place. When I whistle, you come runnin' in. If she ain't scared out of her wits at the sight, I miss my guess."

"Supposin' she still won't tell us, Chough?"

"Then we'll tell her we'll have to take it out of her hide, her and her daughter's!"

The men laughed, as if he had told a good joke. Gildaen's whiskers quivered at their coldbloodedness. Hickory came forward.

"I do not like this plan," he said in his slow, deliberate way. "I will not fight women. I will not hurt a woman."

Chough said soothingly, "Don't be frettin', Hickory; she'll be too scared to put up a fuss. These widows always

have plenty put away. And don't forget," he added, a
wicked gleam in his eyes, "whose side of the law yer on
now!"

The big man turned away. There was more laughter,
the men nudging each other and talking, obviously about
Hickory. Gildaen thought it odd that Hickory would allow them to laugh at him, and there was something shame-
faced about the way he retreated from Chough's eyes that
made Gildaen wonder more than ever about the place
that Hickory held in this robber band.

The prince ran back to the corner he had slept in, pretending to search in the straw for something he had
dropped. He bent low and, turning his back to the others,
whispered to Gildaen, "Follow us. When we are close to
the cottage, you must run ahead with all your speed and
warn the Widow Flann!"

That was all he had time to say, for the others were
ready to leave, and Chough was addressing Evon.

"You're not safe to leave behind, I'll be bound. Take
him in tow, Hickory, and watch out he don't slip away.
I don't trust him any more'n I did last night."

The robbers set out in high spirits, talking and boasting
of what they would do with the widow's gold. Evon and
Hickory walked just behind the others, through the courtyard, over the splintered drawbridge, down the dusty,
wagon-rutted road to the east.

Gildaen stayed well behind until the men were down
the road. He hopped into the garden and looked past the
castle toward the Lower Wood. In that moment he said
farewell to his home. He knew that he could stay behind,
forget Evon, and never worry again about the robbers. Yet
even as he considered this possibility, he brushed it aside.
For the first time in his brief life, he felt of importance.
He had been given a task, and, like it or not, he had to

perform it. "I shall have to hurry a bit," he thought as he
dashed across the drawbridge and into the weeds and
grasses beside the roadway. In a few minutes he had caught
up with the stragglers. Evon and Hickory were now in
the midst of the company, both looking grim and unhappy. While the men found the walking difficult in the
rutted road, he saw that he would have no trouble keeping
up with them in the wild grasses that bordered the farm
fields they were passing.

The weather still held good, but Gildaen remembered
the warning of the birds the previous night. Bad weather
was on the way; he sensed the coming change, too. Now
and again a stiff breeze blew up, swirling the dust into
the men's faces, making them cough and choke and be-
griming them further. The sun shone fitfully, covered
every few minutes by dark clouds blowing west. It seemed
to Gildaen almost as if the wind were trying to blow
them back, away from their intended mischief. They
passed one small farmyard after another. The farmers
looked them over, suspicious and fearful as they strode by.
They held back their furiously barking dogs, not wanting
trouble with such an unsavory-looking crew. Gildaen was
glad he had chosen the less settled side of the road to
travel. His heart beat fast when he saw the dogs straining
at their leashes, but his luck held and none of the dogs
were freed.

Gildaen was now much farther from his home than he
had ever ventured before. In the past, the first farmer's
cottage had served as a barrier to further exploring. He
had been chased by the farmer's dogs on that occasion,
and only a long run through bog and brier had shaken
them off and sent them home. He was a bit disappointed
that the countryside looked just the same as it did around
the Lower Wood. Somehow, he had believed that every-

thing would be different out of the sight of his familiar surroundings.

Chough stopped the men not too far away from a cottage, small, low, like the others they had passed, except perhaps that there was a neglected look to the place. The farmyard was small, and only a flock of chickens scratching for food and two grazing cows were to be seen near the house.

"That's the place, mates!" warned Chough. "No more noise now, you hear? I'll whistle when I want you in a hurry!"

As Chough was giving these instructions, Gildaen ran ahead as fast as he could go, which was quite fast, for Gildaen prided himself on his sprinting. He had always outrun his fellows in a short dash. He sped through the fields, wondering what he should do when he arrived at the cottage. All his life he had been frightened of humans, and before his meeting with Evon, his greatest care had been to stay away from them altogether. He crossed the field where the cows were grazing, spurted past the surprised chickens and a preening rooster who squawked, "What manners!" after him, and up to the door. With his large hind legs he thumped on the door and waited.

The door was opened by a woman in a brown dress and white apron with a kerchief tied around her head. She looked about and, seeing no one, was about to close the door again. Gildaen took advantage of her hesitation and hopped past her skirt into the house.

"Widow Flann," he said, almost breathless.

"Who is there?" asked the poor woman, not knowing whether to be more frightened or surprised by the knock and the small voice that came from behind her.

"Please look down, Widow Flann, and please don't be too upset!" begged Gildaen, still trying to catch his breath.

When she saw the rabbit there in her cottage, the woman was struck dumb for a moment. Then she sank down on her knees.

"Are you a spirit?" she whispered. "Please do not harm us! I have done no one a wrong!"

"Ma'am, I am no spirit or any such thing. I am only a woodland rabbit and no more than I seem. But the power of my good master, the Prince Evon, has helped me to understand and to speak to all beings, and so I am able to talk to you."

"Isn't your master an evil man then, a sorcerer, to have such power?" she cried.

"No, no! He is good, that I promise you! He has sent me ahead to warn you. You must run away. Right now! Leave whatever you are doing, take your daughter, and get away while you can. A band of robbers is on the way. First, one man will come to search out your gold, and if he cannot find it, the lot of them will try to make you tell them where you have hidden it!"

"Alas," she said sadly, rising again. "The rumor of the gold! The villagers are full of stories and idle suspicions of witchcraft, magic, and buried treasure. I knew someone would believe it. My poor foolish husband believed in such things. He was always going off to look for gold and buried hoards. I pleaded with him. I told him that if we worked hard, had plentiful harvests, and tended our animals, we would have enough for our needs, but no, he never listened. He went off every time he heard a story of a treasure to be found, and he came back weary, often sick, for me to nurse. Never did he find so much as a silver coin." She shook her head sorrowfully. "And now that he is dead, the story of our hidden gold will not die with him."

"Then you have no gold?" Gildaen asked, surprised. He had thought Chough's story was true.

"No gold, no silver, hardly a copper coin. The harvest from a few fields, our cows and chickens, and the help of a neighbor—these feed us, and that is all we have."

"But they will not believe you. You must run away!" urged Gildaen.

"Come with me," she said. At the back of the cottage a curtain hung. The woman drew it back and put a finger to her lips. In a bed lay a girl, of eleven or twelve years of age, her eyes closed. She turned her head restlessly, and he could see that her lips were parched and dry. Her long dark hair made her small face paler by contrast.

"This is my daughter, Fara. She has been shaking with fever for two days. I have nursed her through the night, and I am glad that she is resting a little. You see why I cannot run away." She clasped her hands. "There is no escape for us," she said brokenly.

They heard someone whistling outside, then a knock on the cottage door.

The woman turned to Gildaen in anguish. "What am I to do?" she whispered.

"My master will think of something," he whispered. "But I have a thought that may do us some good. Let the man in. Don't let him know you suspect him. And then, tell him—come closer!" He whispered his idea into her ear.

"I'll trust you," she said. "Hide there beneath the bed. I'll do just as you say."

Gildaen crept under the bed, and the Widow Flann drew the curtain.

There was another knock on the door, louder and more impatient.

"I'm coming," called the Widow Flann, hastening to open the latch.

"Good day to you, ma'am," said Chough in his smoothest voice.

"Good day to you, sir," she replied.

"I've been on the road since break o' day," he said, trying to sound like the honest workman he was not. "May I sit by your fire and rest?" he asked.

"I'm sorry, sir," she said, "but I have nothing to offer a stranger. We are poor folk here."

"Who asked for anythin'? Just a chance to sit is all I ask." He grinned at her, pushed the door open, and boldly looked around. He sat himself down on the stool before the hearth.

"That's better, far better, Widow Flann," he said, rubbing his hands. "Now, bring out yer ale."

"You know my name?" she asked, pretending to be surprised.

"I know everythin' about you, Widow Flann," he said with yet another unpleasant grin.

"I have fresh buttermilk. Though you do have a rude tongue, you have made yourself my guest." She handed him a mug of buttermilk, and he drained it.

"A woman with your means should have ale, I think, and live in a better place than this little hole that even a hedgepig would turn up his nose at!"

"I live as well as I can, sir, with what I have," she replied, a little of her anger showing in her voice.

"You should use your gold, woman, not hide it in the ground where thieves might find it," he said menacingly, staring her down.

"You speak strangely. I have no gold. My poor dead husband dreamed of gold and talked of nothing else, but he never found any—nor will you!"

"So that's how it's to be, eh? We'll soon find out. Maybe your daughter will help us," he mocked, grinning horribly. "Where is she, Widow Flann?"

The widow walked to the curtain and drew it back, showing him the girl tossing feverishly in bed.

"There she is, you wicked knave! She has the plague, the deadly plague that has killed many hundreds of good honest folk, and you, you rogue who have been in this house and had drink from her cup—aye, that was her cup you drank from!—you will soon have it, too!"

Chough's face turned deadly pale. He stepped back toward the door, shielding his face from the sight of the girl. "No," he stammered, "no, no, no, not the plague!"

The Widow Flann stepped toward him holding up the mug.

"Soon you will be sweating and fevered, and who will tend you, I'd like to know!"

He ran out the door, wiping his mouth, babbling of the plague as he ran. His men stood up in the fields, astounded to see their leader seemingly out of his wits.

Gildaen ran from his hiding place and watched Chough dashing for the road. He saw the prince raise his arm and point it at the running figure, fleeing in such terror. As Chough stumbled onward, he began to change. He grew smaller and darker; his wildly waving arms became black wings. His feet took on the shape of claws, and he left the road altogether, his flapping wings bearing him aloft. He had become a crow, screeching and cawing. Evon turned and with a sweeping circle of his arm pointed at the other members of the robber band. Chough's men shriveled quickly and took wing, until the fields were deserted except for the prince and Hickory, looking up at the sky, and the two cows who continued to browse.

Overhead, the flock of crows circled, cawing and wheeling above the cottage. A strong storm wind was blowing from the east. The birds rose higher, buffeted by the coming storm, and fled with the scudding clouds toward the northwest.

FARA FLANN

ILDAEN WATCHED THE CROWS GROW SMALLER
and smaller in the darkened sky until they
were specks in the distance. He raced across
the farmyard to the place where Hickory
and the prince stood shading their eyes with
their hands, looking at the fleeing birds. Then he came to
an abrupt halt, almost tumbling over at the prince's feet.

"Evon! You saved the widow and her daughter!"

The prince shook his head. "I was not sure until the
very last that I could do it. I was afraid that nothing would
happen. But I would like to know what part you played
in Chough's haste. He seemed in a great hurry to get away
from the widow and her gold!"

39

Now that the danger was over, Gildaen felt quite pleased with himself for his part in the rescue. He tried to speak modestly, though, as his mother had counseled him.

"I know that humans have suffered much from the disease they call the plague," he explained. "My mother and father often talked of the time when the farmhouses in our part of the land were deserted. Many people died of this plague. The roads were filled with those who were trying to run away from it. The widow's daughter is sick and fevered. I hoped that Chough would be afraid if he thought that he might catch the plague from her."

Evon smiled grimly. "He was eager to save his skin, I am sure," he said.

Hickory had stepped away from them. He stared at them with growing astonishment.

"The rabbit speaks!" he said. "You must indeed be a sorcerer," he said to Evon.

"Perhaps I am, Hickory," Evon answered. "Are you afraid?"

The big man shook his head slowly. "No, I do not fear you. Maybe I should, but I do not. You are a good-hearted lad. I knew that when first I laid eyes on you. I am not sure who or what you are, but, strange to say, I have no fear of you."

Hickory's words were almost drowned out by the howling of the wind, which blew more fiercely every moment. The clouds grew blacker, and a cold rain that was part sleet pelted them.

"Let us go in!" shouted Evon, and without any further attempt at talk, they ran for the cottage.

The Widow Flann met them at the door. "I've the cows and chickens in the barn, and here you are still standing in the wet. Come in, come in!" she urged them.

"Which one is your friend?" she asked Gildaen.

"This is Prince Evon, ma'am," said Gildaen, putting his paw on Evon's boot.

"I am more grateful to you, young sir, than words can tell for your warning, and for the help of this rabbit. You are welcome to the shelter of my poor house. Take off your cloaks and boots and come to the fire. Bless me, but you're wet!"

It was only too true. There were three puddles on the floor where they stood. The woman took their cloaks and sodden boots and pulled a second stool close to the fire for Hickory. She fetched a soft cloth for Gildaen and draped it over him.

"Sir rabbit, will you let me dry your fur before you take a chill?" she asked gently.

"Thank you, ma'am," he answered, and allowed her to lift him onto her lap. With great care she dried the fine, soft fur of his chest and the rougher brown fur on his back. Gildaen marveled that he felt no fear of this woman. She seemed to understand that he was shy and wary, and she took pains to see that none of her movements startled him. This was the second human he had decided he could trust.

"May I ask you, young sir," she said, addressing Evon, "if my eyes played me a trick? Did you have something to do with changing those men into birds?"

Evon replied in a serious voice, "I changed them into likenesses of what they are—robbers. Now everybody who sees them will recognize them as thieves. They may steal corn from a farmer's field, but they cannot do any real mischief!"

Hickory was warming his hands at the fire. At these words he turned his head and looked at the prince.

"Why," he asked slowly, "did you not change me along with the others?"

Gildaen had been asking himself that question. Hickory was easily the most powerful of the robbers. Chough had trusted him to watch Evon, and he had obeyed Chough's orders, even to coming along this morning with the intention of robbing the widow. Gildaen was uneasy to be within reach of those huge arms.

Evon smiled. It was an easy smile, and a friendly one.

"Hickory," he said, "I am no more afraid of you than you are of me. You are no robber. I see that you are neither crafty nor cruel. I do not think you have harmed anyone. Tell me the truth: has not Chough forced you to go along with him and do his bidding?"

A look of sorrow came into Hickory's eyes. "Aye, Evon lad, that is so. I thought I had no choice but to stay with him."

"You poor man," clucked the Widow Flann.

"Stay your tale a while—until I bring you all something to keep body and soul together."

She set Gildaen down before the fire and bustled about the little room fetching food.

"Here is buttermilk from the crock, bread—would that I had a fine wheaten loaf to offer!—my own good cheese, and a mite of sausage. And for you, master rabbit, I have parsnips and carrots. Does that suit you?" she asked anxiously.

They assured her that they were more than pleased with their fare.

"I am wondering," asked Hickory, turning to Evon, "if you can use your powers to conjure food for this good woman's larder?"

"I doubt it," answered Evon. "I have tried before, but I shall try again. Nothing lost in that!"

They watched with silent interest as he stared at the meal set before them. Gildaen saw that both the widow and Hickory anticipated the arrival of a magical feast at any moment, but after long minutes of waiting, Evon smiled and said, apologetically, "I am very sorry, my friends, but I cannot seem to do anything about the food. It would seem that there are well-defined limits to my powers."

"Never mind, lad," said Hickory. "It was a foolish thought of mine."

A low moan from behind the curtain made the widow jump up immediately and go to her daughter.

"What can I bring you, Fara, my dear. Will you drink some water?"

The girl turned her head toward them, her eyes wide and bright with fever.

"Mother, I heard thunder and the sleet beating on the roof. I thought it was falling on me, but I am so hot and dry, and it hasn't cooled me at all, Mother, not at all." She stared at the group around her bed, her eyes lingering on Gildaen.

"Who are those strangers, Mother?"

"Friends, dear," she replied soothingly. "Friends they are, of mine and of yours, though they do look a queer lot. Lie quiet, Fara love, and I'll put a cool cloth on your forehead."

The prince came and stroked her forehead.

"Oh," she murmured. "That feels good! Mother, his hand is gentle and cool, cool as well water in the summer."

She closed her eyes, sighing contentedly.

The widow said, "I have been fair out of my wits trying to do what is best for her. Since yesterday she will not eat and wakes only to ask for drink. I have soothed her with cooling cloths on her forehead. She talks on and on about the heat. When you put your hand on her forehead, she smiled and looked glad for the first time since she fell sick.

I can't bear to see her so pale and still!" She held Fara's hand in hers.

"I think I may be able to help," said Evon comfortingly. "Have you dried herbs?"

"To be sure! But none of them has availed."

"Let us try," said Evon. "Bring sweet balm and vervain, if you have them."

She nodded and hastened to bring them to him, together with her wooden mortar and pestle.

"We will make an electuary for her," he said as he ground the herbs to a powder. He added a few drops of boiling water, and a fresh, pleasing aroma was wafted from the mixture. Widow Flann brought out her honey crock for the prince, who spooned in enough to make a syrupy paste. Finally he minced fine and then ground a bit of the stramony root he had gathered in the old castle garden and added it.

He took Fara's hands and rubbed them gently until she opened her eyes. This time she smiled back at him wanly but confidently.

He handed the bowl and a spoon to her, and she took the medicine without a word. Her mother offered her water, and she drank thirstily.

"This should cool you and soothe you and give you quiet sleep," said Evon.

"Your eyes," she said softly, "they aren't like the eyes of any boy I've ever met. They are older. And kinder, too, I think, but different, anyway. Who are you?"

"I wish I knew, Fara. You know as much as anyone and more than most could guess."

She sighed, turned her head, and in a few moments slipped into sleep.

The prince raised a finger to his lips, and very quietly they withdrew. The Widow Flann pulled the curtain.

"When she wakes, you will see that she is much improved," Evon said.

"I don't know whether to cry, I'm that relieved," the Widow Flann said, "or to laugh, I'm so merry! I feel as if a great load were lifted from me, young man; and now you must come and finish your meal."

The wind, which had abated for a time, began to wail and howl, pelting the cottage with hail.

"We're in for it!" said their hostess. "The first storm of winter is here, and you must stay snug and warm with us."

"We would not think of staying with you longer than we must," replied the prince politely.

"Hush, now!" she said indignantly. "I wouldn't turn out my worst enemy in weather like this. Surely I'll not let those to whom I'm deep in debt face the storm! No more talk of leaving, I beg you. I'll make a kettle of soup to warm us all this evening," she said cheerfully.

From her tiny storeroom she fetched more vegetables, a few bones, a chunk of salted meat, barley, and dried herbs and busied herself with preparing the soup.

The others watched her in silence. Now that Fara was sleeping peacefully, they found themselves short of conversation. Evon seemed to be waiting for Hickory to speak, and Hickory sat staring into the fire as if his attention were held by something far away. Gildaen did not feel it his place to say anything.

Only the Widow Flann seemed unconcerned by the silence that had overtaken them. She hummed contentedly as if she were accustomed to entertaining homeless princes and talking rabbits and robbers in her house every day of the year.

The smell of soup filled the cottage. Gildaen was very drowsy and decided that a nap before dinner was not a bad idea. He fell asleep listening to the wind.

HICKORY

HE FIRST THOUGHT THAT CAME TO HIM WHEN
he awoke was that he had been trapped and
brought to the bad end his mother had fore-
told. The pot bubbling on the fire reminded
him uncomfortably of tales about those of
his relatives who had become someone's lunch or dinner.
The Widow Flann's voice broke into these odious thoughts
and reminded him of where he was.

"You're awake, I see, master rabbit?"

"Yes, ma'am," was all he could bring himself to answer
as he watched her stirring the cook pot.

"I was right, you see. The snow has come." She added
wood to the fire and sighed. "Ah well," she said, "the

winter's here, whether one likes it or not, and I am glad
I have wood enough this year to last us through it, thanks
to my good neighbor, Farmer Liddle."

She stirred the soup and said, "The barley is almost
done, and the soup will soon be ready. Then we will have
a fine supper."

"Mother," came a soft voice from behind the curtain.
The next moment the curtain was pulled back by Fara
herself. She looked out at them, her face still pale, but
with clear eyes and a smile.

"Fara, darling, will you eat something?" her mother
asked, crossing the room and hugging the girl.

"I smelled the soup, Mother, right into my dream. The
smell woke me up and made me feel how hungry I am. I
could eat a whole pot!"

With a glad face the Widow Flann filled a bowl with
hot soup.

Evon took his bowl and his stool across the room to
keep Fara company as she sat in bed hungrily eating her
soup.

"I see you are feeling better!"

"Yes, thank you, much better. I am sorry I forgot to ask
before, but what is your name?"

"I am called Evon."

"But that is not your real name." She said it as a state-
ment, not as a question.

He shook his head. "You said before that I was not what
I seemed, and that was true. Do you know any more about
me, Fara?"

"No," she said with a smile. "I only know that I like
you! Have you bumped your head and forgotten who you
are?"

"Perhaps. Gildaen and I set out to discover who I really

am; then we fell into an adventure—or should I say we
were pulled in by Hickory over there!—and here we are."

At these words Hickory turned his head away and set
down his bowl. Fara was too interested in questioning
Evon to notice, but Gildaen saw him.

"Gildaen is your rabbit?" she asked.

"Not mine, Fara. He belongs to no one but himself.
He wanted to come with me."

Gildaen felt shy as Fara stared at him.

"And you can really speak?" she asked in wonder.

He hopped closer. Her eyes encouraged him.

"Prince Evon gave me that gift—of course, we don't
know that he is a prince. We're calling him Evon after
my eldest brother," he confided.

"I see," she said. "And this other friend of yours, Evon,
this Hickory, who is he?"

Hickory remained seated near the hearth, his eyes cast
down. Gildaen decided to answer for him.

"This is one of the robber band who came here looking
for your gold."

"Gold?" Her eyes widened. "We never had any gold."
She gazed at Hickory again. "There must be some mistake,
Gildaen. That man is not a robber!"

Hickory met her eyes for the first time. He answered
slowly, as if the words came painfully to him: "I was one
of their band."

"Were you with them long?" she inquired.

"No, Mistress Fara, that I was not!" he said, his voice
booming out with the vehemence of his feeling.

Fara coaxed as if she were the older of the two. "Come,
Hickory, you must tell us about it."

He shook his head unhappily. "Talking makes no difference. Talking won't change what's past and done."

Gildaen suddenly felt pity for this big man who sat in misery, hunched over his stool.

"Hickory," he said timidly, "if you let us share your trouble, maybe it will seem lighter to you."

A slow smile spread across Hickory's broad face.

"I cannot get used to hearing a rabbit sit and speak his piece. It's beyond me!" He was silent for several moments. They could tell that he was trying to decide whether to take them into his confidence.

"I've not been with good folk for too long," he said, slapping his knee with his big hand. "I will tell you how I came to be in the company of Chough and those others.

"Chough says I am one of them, an outlaw, but if it were not for a black-hearted rogue, I would never have set eyes on the lot of them! I grew up in the service of the old king. My father was his master of the hunt, and from my youth I was trained in that craft, to track and to stalk, to use bow, spear, and knife.

"I remember the young King Justin, he that sits now on the throne, when he was a pert, wee lad, standing by my father's side in the courtyard, watching our practice with the crossbow. Evon—you have a look about you that 'minds me of him. In faith, I thought for a time in the old castle that maybe you *were* him, until you spoke up and faced out the rascals. King Justin was like kin of my own to me, though I did not forget ever that he was a prince born to rule. I made his first bow for him. 'Twas I who took him first into the forest to listen and to learn.

"Last spring when he had just come into his fifteenth year, the old king died of a sudden; he was a noble king, slow to anger, kindly, and a fair man. I knew that the boy was sorrowing for his father—he's had no mother since he was ten. He had to leave his boy's ways and act the king.

His father's counselor, the Lord Royce, was good to him, and I did what I could to help him, little though it was. We had fine hunting days together then, and he was carefree, as much as a young king could be, until Grimald came!"

"Who is he?" Fara asked.

Evon said, half to himself, "I know that name. I cannot remember in what connection."

"Would that I had never heard it!" said Hickory. "He is called the Lord of the Bower. There are strange rumors about his castle in the north. It is said that he has a magical garden in which he grows herbs and poisons. I believe that! Nothing was the same from the time he and his liegemen came to court. They said they came only to show their respect for the new king, but they did not leave. The Lord of the Bower goes off to his poisons in the north every few months, but back he comes, like a sickness, to wither my lord, King Justin."

"What is he like?" asked the widow.

"His age is hard to tell. He does not stoop or seem lacking in strength, though his beard is gray. His eyes are hard and cold—like stones, I thought, the minute I laid eyes on him. People are afraid of him. I thought my master would shy from him, but the villain took pains to charm my lord. When the Lord of the Bower speaks, you must listen, whether you will or not, even while he stares you down with those flinty eyes of his.

"It was his care to woo the boy from his friends. Every week the influence of Lord Royce grew less, and every week Grimald's was greater. He tried to keep the king from my company. He flattered the poor boy until he hardly knew up from down! Still, my master seemed to like me near him and to trust me as much as ever. 'Hick-

ory,' he'd say, 'you are as stout a fellow and as good a
huntsman as ever a king had to serve him.'

"One morning before sunrise, I was shaken from my
sleep by two varlets of Grimald and brought, without even
a chance to wash my face or tidy my clothes, to my master's
bedchamber. I'd have thrown the both of them out the
door if they hadn't told me the king himself wanted me
at once. His chamberlain was helping him dress, and
standing by was Grimald, his eyes gleaming with some
secret pleasure. The king, poor lad, looked miserable
enough!

" 'Hickory,' he said, speaking slow, 'have a look at this.'
His squire brought out one of my heavy hunting spears.

" 'It's my prize spear, my lord!' said I, surprised to see
it there—I as innocent as a baby and as easily led to harm.

" 'One of the great stags of the forest was found this
night dying in a thicket, this spear through him.'

" 'Your majesty,' said I, still puzzled, 'we did not hunt
yesterday.'

" 'No, Hickory, we did not. But Lord Grimald, whose
men found the stag and finished him, says that you yourself were hunting, or poaching I should say, and that your
quarry escaped you before you could finish him.'

" 'My lord!' said I, nailed to the spot with amaze, not
able to think of what to say to so gross a lie.

" 'It is your spear, Hickory, as you have yourself confessed. No other can wield it, so heavy is it made. By the
laws of the kingdom, this offense of poaching calls for
death,' he said, trying not to let his voice quaver. 'But
thinking upon your years of service, and those of your late
father before you, I have decided'—and here he stopped
to take a breath—'not to do you bodily harm. I sentence
you to banishment for life, Hickory. You are outside the

protection of my law, and you are acquitted of your fealty
to me. If you are taken within my domain after today, the
punishment is death. Now, go!"

"I could see he was on the point of weeping. The varlets
of Grimald took my arms and led me away. I could easily
have shaken them off, but I knew my lord would think
the worse of me for flouting his word. I was allowed to
take only the clothes on my back, but I slipped my hunting
knife under my jerkin. I was led through the courtyard, a
page walking before me, calling out the king's sentence to
the palace folk. My friends, the armorers, the grooms, my
good companions, muttered and looked black, but none
of them could help me. I was taken past the gates and onto
the forest path, and there I was left alone. I looked back
and felt that I must still be asleep and dreaming. I walked
into the forest without a thought of where I was or where
I would go. I let my legs carry me on, and never did I stop
until I could walk no farther. I found a mossy bank and
rested against the trunk of a tree. I had come farther into
the forest than I had ever gone before. Next thing I
thought was that it didn't matter that I was lost since I
had no home to go back to. Never again! That was hard
to bear. I would have bawled like a baby if I had not been
schooled all my life to a hunter's ways. I could not cry,
and I could not think. I had nothing to eat, no drink to
quench my thirst. I was as weary and heartsick as a man
has ever been.

"I got up and walked on, not giving a thought to where
I was going. I would have been easy prey for any wild
creature of the forest. The light began to fail, and still I
stumbled along until I was ready to fall to my knees and
sleep. But the ground was covered with brush, and there
were bramble bushes everywhere. I kept walking until it

was full dark. Then I saw the light of a fire ahead, and I made for it. I gave no thought to the manner of men who'd be keeping their camp in the wilds of the wood. I walked right in amongst 'em, glad to find human company. They were roasting chunks of meat, passing the wineskin, at their ease. When they saw me, they jumped up and drew their knives. They tried to grab me and pull me down, but since I have some little strength in these arms"— Gildaen looked at those mighty thews with respect—"I threw a few of them here and there instead, until their leader called out to them to move away from me. I didn't like the man. His face had a look of the weasel about it. But he spoke me fair, asked me my name and what I wanted of them. I told them my story, but I could see that they didn't believe me. The leader—he was Chough —winked at me and said that I'd been greatly wronged, at which the others gave a shout of laughter. He told me that all of them had been wronged by the young king and his father before him and that they lived as best they could, foraging in the forest in the summer. He made place for me by the fire and gave me food and drink. I did not know then that they were robbers, or I'd have walked away into the forest and taken my chances with the beasts."

Hickory stopped and turned to each of them. "I should have seen that they were worthless and bad-hearted, but that night I was glad to be with 'em, glad to find a place to lay my head. Summer was going, and there was a chill in the air you could feel. Next morning Chough told me over and over again how meanly I'd been used. He asked me to join his men.

" 'We're good fellows all,' he said, 'a bit rough some are, but you'll soon be used to our ways.'

"We found game enough in the woods those days

(Gildaen's ears went down, and he crept closer to Evon), but nights were getting cold, and we left the forest to seek a snugger camp. We foraged through the midland wood in the first months of fall until we came to the castle in which we took you prisoner, Evon. Our food was running low, and Chough was showing his true ways. The others fought among themselves. When you came, Evon, and I saw how they planned to use you, I knew that what I had begun to suspicion about these men was true. They were wicked rogues. I saw your courage, the way you talked and acted, and I knew then that they were base cowards. You are very like the young king in some ways, yet you are sure where he is unsure, and you know far more than your years tell. When I heard their plan to rob the widow, I listened, wondering the while how I might prevent them, for that I intended to do, though I think it would have cost me my life in the end." He looked at them imploringly. "I have been brought low, but never would I harm the weak or innocent. I am ashamed to have been one of them."

He bowed his head and went down on his knees before Evon. "You, young sir, if you will let me, I will serve until I die."

Evon touched him on the shoulder. "Rise, Hickory. Your heart, as this girl has seen, is good. Talk no more of service to me. I do not even know my own right name, and though I will gladly accept good friends, I cannot have servitors. You are your own man, and any allegiance you wish to give must still be sworn to your own king. This Grimald has led him far astray, even as Chough sought to lead you."

"Grimald—that black-hearted knave!" roared Hickory. "My blood runs hot with rage when I think of him. He will lead my young master to destruction! Now it comes to my mind that Chough knew of him, too. When first I mentioned the Lord of the Bower, I remember he gave me a black, sour kind of look and a shudder. He told me, though now I know not whether to believe him, that he had once been an underling of the Lord of the Bower, but he cursed him and said that he had been dismissed from his service."

"Evil birds of a feather do indeed flock together, Hickory, and though they part company, these folk find each other again. The more I think on your story, the less I like it. If this Grimald is as evil as you think him, he will soon rule the kingdom in reality, though your king may still sit upon the throne and seem to govern. No one will be safe, especially those who have no guile to protect them."

Evon turned to Gildaen. "I believe now," he said, "that our best plan is to follow the course on which we seem to be set. I am no closer to remembering who I am, but I have a memory, or think I do, of this Lord of the Bower, this Grimald, a fleeting recollection that he and I have met before. The tale Hickory has told makes me believe we must find out more about this man, and, in doing so, it may be that we can help you, Hickory. We must try to clear your name."

Hickory shook his head sadly. "I can never show my face in the king's presence again. How can I prove my innocence? I could not do it then, on the spot, and I know not to this moment how I could have done better. I am slow to think and to speak, though not to act, when need arises."

"Nonetheless," replied Evon firmly, "we will find a way to help you."

"You mean," Gildaen asked, "we are going to seek out the king?" The prospect was exciting, but he was already sure he did not want to make the acquaintance of the man called the Lord of the Bower.

"Yes, we must go to his court."

"But where is the king?" Gildaen asked.

"Far away, master rabbit," answered Hickory. "We are many leagues from Castelmaine, my home, where the king spends half the year. The king has gone south to his winter palace of Hearthfire. He will stay there for the hunting until after the spring snows are gone, and then he and his court will return to Castelmaine."

"Which is the shortest way to Hearthfire from here?" asked Evon.

"Indeed, I can only make a guess," replied Hickory.

"A good week's journey by wagon," the Widow Flann said. "My sister Wilma and her husband, Walter Walloon, are there now—he is chief cook in the king's kitchens."

"Walter Walloon?" repeated Hickory. "Why I know him, Widow Flann, and your kind sister, too. He is a good man, though he is a great worrier."

"Then you'll have friends there who can help you!" The Widow Flann beamed.

"And how long is the journey?" inquired Evon.

"Walking it, keeping a good pace, I think we might do it in two weeks," Hickory said, "though only strong grown men could keep such a pace, day after day, especially at this season. The wind sweeps far inland off the sea, and the east wind brings storms to freeze the bones."

"I have a question," said Fara shyly.

They turned to look at her.

"Why can't you fly there?" she asked.

"Fly?" said Hickory. "Why, we are not birds, Mistress Fara!"

"But Evon turned the robbers into birds, didn't he? Why can't he turn the three of you into birds? Wouldn't that be the easiest way?"

Evon shook his head. "I've thought of that, Fara. But I'd rather not try it. I know that I can change myself into any shape at will—but more than that I do not know. When I turned the robbers into crows, I was desperate. I did not know whether I *could* change them, yet I had no choice but to try. I do not know if I could change them back to men. Suppose I use my 'magic' on Hickory and Gildaen and then find I cannot undo what I have done?"

"Best not to try," said the Widow Flann.

"Remember that I tried to provide food for us with my powers and couldn't? I think that until I know who I am —and what I am capable of doing—I will use my powers sparingly."

"I have no wish to be a bird," said Hickory with a smile. "I would rather walk!"

Gildaen said nothing, but he was grateful that Evon was not going to turn him into some other creature.

"Whatever plans you have, sirs, must wait," said the Widow Flann with determination. "You can go nowhere today. It is late. The storm is fierce, and you would surely lose your way in this snow and wind."

"We can't burden you further," Evon replied. "There is no room for us here."

"Oh, please stay!" cried Fara. "What if you should come to harm in this weather? And besides, I long to know you better, all of you!"

"Fara is right, good sirs. You might not perish of the cold or the snow, but you would make little headway. Wait here with us. You will not live in luxury, but you will be safe. I have spun and woven winter wear for my neighbor, Farmer Liddle, and in return he has given us salted meat and harvested grain enough so that, if we are careful, none of us need fear going hungry. Wait out this storm at least, I beg of you! We would be pleased to have you wait the whole winter through until the roads are passable again and your journey more secure."

Gildaen's short life had known only one previous winter. He remembered with a shiver the trips through the snow to find food, the fear he had felt lest his tracks give him away to a watching enemy, and his happiness when he reached the burrow again to snuggle for warmth against his brothers and sisters. This little house with its cozy room and bright fire gave him something of the same feeling of safety. Yet he knew that if Evon decided to leave, he would follow him out into the winter storm.

Evon's glance fell on him, almost as if he had heard Gildaen's thoughts.

"It would be prudent, I admit, for us to stay until the storm abates. But we can't deprive you of privacy and house room, Widow Flann. Is there a place for us in the barn?"

"Now, no such talk, sir! How could I let you stay in the barn while there is room here?"

"Your cows and chickens are quartered there, are they not?"

"Aye, it is dry enough and warm enough, with the hay piled to the rafters. My neighbor, Farmer Liddle, and his man Stave, as I told you, harvested our oats and brought in the hay for us. Thanks be to them, we have grain and our cows have food."

"Then we will be warm and dry there also. Let us go now and see what needs to be done."

Still protesting heartily, the good woman followed them out of doors into the wildly swirling snow. Gildaen rode snug under Evon's cloak, and so he was the only one who was not out of breath and snow-covered when they crowded into the barn.

There were squawks and clucks from the chickens as Hickory stamped his feet free of snow. Gildaen listened to their comments on the intruders.

"Why don't they make haste to close the door! We'll freeze to death!" snapped the rooster.

"Who are the strangers?"

"That big one will trample us, I know it!"

"I don't like it! I don't like it!"

And the little chicks in their high-pitched voices called, "Mother, Mother, Mother!" as they hastened to hide beneath the feathers of the three hens.

The two black-and-white cows merely stared at them in astonishment. Gildaen saw that they were very shy.

"This will do nicely," said Evon, looking around. To their hostess he added, "We will make fine beds in the hay tonight."

He set Gildaen down and started smoothing the high-piled hay into a place for their beds. Hickory joined him at this work.

"Well, then, if your minds are set on the barn, you are more than welcome to it for as long as you like."

She bustled out, leaving them to their task.

The chickens burst into discussion again when she left.

"Will they be staying here, then?"

"Who are these men? Why do they have that rabbit with them?"

"Perhaps he is their dinner for tomorrow," commented the fattest hen.

Gildaen was indignant. "Dinner indeed!" he snorted. "Perhaps *you* are their dinner tomorrow!"

There was an instant of horrified silence at these words, and then the entire flock ran about the barn, shrieking and squawking, looking for hiding places.

Evon laughed aloud, but he said to Gildaen, "See what your idle words have done? Why not tell them the truth and quiet their fears?"

Gildaen sighed. "Ah, very well. I am sorry, Evon, but you must admit I was provoked."

He made a graceful leap that carried him high onto the hay.

"Come back!" he called out. "No one here will harm you. This man who looks so big and fierce to you"—and he nodded toward Hickory—"is a kind man. He is not looking for a chicken dinner tonight. Nor is this boy Evon. He can work mighty deeds and he can talk to you himself, for he understands the tongues of all creatures, and he has given me that knowledge, too."

The rooster strutted forward from the cow stalls where he had been listening.

"I certainly am not afraid," he announced. "I want you to know, you furry burrow-hider, that I could, if I wished, peck and scratch you until you would be thankful to escape alive. What is your name?" he demanded regally.

"Gildaen."

"I am Chanticleer XII," the rooster said proudly. "My father and my grandsires before him have ruled this roost. I am also called Chanticleer the Magnificent," he added in a smug voice.

"Good Chanticleer," said Evon to the rooster. "I give you my word that we will respect your rights and your sovereignty here. We are travelers in need of a place to stay, and we thought to impose upon your courtesy. May we share your quarters for a time?"

The rooster was much mollified by these gentle words and by the manner of their speaker.

"I have your word that you will harm none of us, nor stay longer than you must?"

"You have my word."

"Very well," said the rooster.

After some coaxing by Chanticleer, the flock emerged and soon were unconcernedly feeding and preening, chattering away with scarcely a glance at the strangers.

"How long will we stay here?" asked Hickory as they poked hay into the few small crevices where the wind could whistle in.

"At first I thought that we should be on our way tomorrow. But the Widow Flann is right. We could not go far. Gildaen would not enjoy traveling now, would you?" he teased, tossing a handful of hay at the rabbit. "I think," Evon continued, "that we will stay through the worst of the winter, and while we are here, we can help the good widow and her daughter put their farm to rights, as much as we can."

"Yes," agreed Hickory. "I saw tasks which need doing, both in the house and out here."

"I am glad that we are staying for a while," said Gildaen, settling down gratefully in the hay.

QUIET DAYS AND
NEW PLANS

O THE WINTER DAYS PASSED BY. HICKORY AND
Evon shoveled snow and kept open the paths
around the farm, and they worked on the
barn, slowly making it as snug and warm
and weather-tight as any such building could
be. Chanticleer had been suspicious at first, but when he
saw how much improved his quarters were, his attitude

changed. He and Gildaen also took to having long talks
—often arguments—on many subjects.

The meals together they all looked forward to. They
were a contented company as they gathered for their
supper of salt meat, bread, and cheese. Gildaen was satisfied with his ration of vegetables from the root cellar,
although he missed the fresh greens of spring and summer.
For a special treat, Hickory often cut for him branches
of poplar or willow, so that he might gnaw to his heart's
content. They stayed together for a short time after this
meal, the Widow Flann and Fara sewing and mending by
the sputtering light of a wick floating in tallow. The
Widow Flann often spoke of her neighbor, the farmer,
William Liddle, telling them of his many kindnesses. "I
wonder that he's not been here," she said on many an
evening. "I would worry about his health if I did not
know that he's spent many a winter before this in the
village with his kinfolk. There's not much at his farm for
him to do once the snow falls; all's well ordered and his
work is done. His man Stave can feed the stock. Still, I
wish he had sent us word of his going," and she would
pause in her work and sigh.

Hickory worked at fashioning a willow basket for Gildaen to ride in during the journey to come. Sometimes
they sang together, or traded stories, but more often they
fell a-yawning and said early good nights. In this fashion
their days turned into weeks, while the long dark of
winter kept them from thinking of the parting soon to
come.

One day in early February as they sat at their midday
meal, there came a knock at the door. They had not seen
a living soul since Chough and his robber band had fled
from them, and so they were still with surprise for a mo-

ment. Gildaen recovered first, leaping behind the stack of firewood, where he could see but not be seen.

The knock came again, louder and more insistent.

"Why, I'll wager that is Farmer Liddle at the door," said the Widow Flann, recollecting herself. "He is the neighbor I've told you of who has helped us so often in the past. Indeed, without you here, I should have thought his absence long."

She opened the door a crack, was reassured, and opened it wide to the man standing on the threshold.

"Welcome, William Liddle!" she said heartily. "You have been a stranger these months."

The man in the doorframe had a round face, cheeks red from the cold, and a shock of dark hair turning to gray.

"Thank you, Millie," he said, stepping in with his cloak snow-covered. He paused and looked at the assembled group in astonishment.

"Why, who are these?" he asked. He looked by no means pleased to see Evon and Hickory seated there.

"We are travelers, Master Liddle, caught by the first snowstorm. The Widow Flann kindly gave us shelter, and we have been earning our keep until the road is fit for travel and we can be on our way again."

"So that's the way of it," the farmer said, his face clearing. "Well, that's a nice bit of company for you and the girl, Millie."

Millicent Flann motioned him to a place at the table and set a bowl of hot soup before him.

"Millie, I came to find if all was well with you and Fara. I took a fall from the loft and twisted my foot. I could do little more than hobble about these many weeks. It has fretted me to sit and do nothing!"

"But, William," she said, "why did you not send Stave to tell me? I would have come to help you!"

"I had sent Stave ahead to my kinfolk in the village. The silly fellow waited for me there until this week, thinking I had made up my mind to stay longer at the farm."

"If only I had known," said the widow.

The farmer rose. "Might I have a word alone with you, Millie?" he said shyly.

She drew her shawl around her shoulders and stepped outside the door with him. The others sat thoughtfully finishing their meal.

In a few moments she returned, her cheeks pink from the cold and her eyes bright. She went over to the fire, holding out her hands to warm them, smiling all the while. Gildaen hopped out from behind the firewood. He was terribly curious to know what Farmer Liddle had said to her in private, and he could see that the others were equally anxious to learn of it.

"Mother!" cried Fara, springing up and hugging her. "Please don't stand and smile to yourself! Tell us what he said to you! Can't you see that we are all dying to know!"

"Oh, well then," she said, laughing still more, "I see that I must tell you now, though I had hoped to have time to think on it myself before I spoke."

She lifted Fara's face so that she could look at her.

"William Liddle has asked me to be his wife. What have you to say to that, Fara love?"

Fara gazed at her mother's expectant face.

"Why, Mother, do you wish to marry him?"

"He is a good man, and a good farmer, too, a man I have liked for many a year. He is fond of you. You were little more than a baby when your father died. You have never known what it is to have the comfort and care that only a father can give you."

"Mother, I see what is in your heart. Marry him and be happy!" She gave her mother another hug.

"My congratulations, madam!" said Evon.

"And mine," said Hickory.

"I am glad, too," said Gildaen.

"When is the wedding to be?" asked Fara.

"Soon," said Millicent Flann. "Spring will be coming, and the wedding over and done with before the season for planting."

"But that leaves little time!" protested Fara.

"For a great wedding feast, aye, Fara. But we shall have only William's kinfolk in the village and a few friends."

"All right, Mother. We will work hard and be ready," said Fara. Mother and daughter smiled at one another. Gildaen was glad to be there to share in their joy.

Each new day was filled with activity, with preparations for the wedding and for the removal to the Liddle farmhouse. Messages were sent back and forth between the two farms by way of Stave, who was always dour and glum, as if his face had never learned the pattern of a smile.

The weather began to turn. There were days when the sun shone for several hours and a few patches of bare earth could be seen. Gildaen went abroad more often on his own, poking his nose here and there around the farmyard.

The fowl in the barn were in a constant flutter of worries. Gildaen had told them of the coming change of residence. At first, they had not believed him.

"Sir," Chanticleer had said, "my fathers from time out of mind have roosted here. I certain shall not leave!"

"You certainly shall," Gildaen answered with satisfaction, "because you have nothing to say about it."

"Impudence!" the rooster said haughtily and, turning his back, strutted away.

One morning when the wedding was but a week away, Farmer Liddle drove over to take Millicent and Fara to the village to buy what the two farms could not supply for the wedding feast.

Gildaen lay hidden behind the barn door. He still had no wish to meet Farmer Liddle and stayed well out of his way.

"Fine horses you have," said Hickory.

"Aye, that they are," the farmer agreed, well pleased. "My second team does well enough for the plowing, but Meg and Sall are my first pair, good as gold they are, and they love an outing. Come along, Millie!" he called. "There's much to be done."

He helped Millicent Flann into the seat beside him. She was dressed in her best, as was Fara.

"Good-bye," called Fara gaily as they started off.

Evon and Hickory waved after them until the wagon was out of sight. Gildaen came to join them.

"I have a feeling of foreboding," said Evon, who still stood staring down the empty road. "I am uneasy."

"I hope you are wrong," said Hickory. "I should not like to see anything mar their happiness."

"Yes," said Evon, "especially now, when we must go."

"Go?" said Gildaen. "Must we leave, then?"

"Our friends will be well cared for," said Hickory, "and I shall have no peace until I can settle with the Lord of the Bower!"

"We will make our farewells before the wedding and go quietly," said Evon. "Have you finished making Gildaen's willow basket, Hickory? There will be times when we'll need to hide him."

"I'll finish it this very day," Hickory said.

Gildaen went to the barn and settled into the straw for a long nap.

It was still early afternoon when the wagon returned. Gildaen heard the horses coming at a good pace, shook himself, and hurried out, staying out of sight. Evon and Hickory came out, but Gildaen noticed that none of the three in the wagon waved or called out. Farmer Liddle's face was grim as he jumped down.

"You are back early," said Hickory.

"What is wrong?" asked Evon.

"Let us talk within, friends," urged Millicent Flann.

Gildaen slipped under Fara's cloak and entered with her. The fire blazed brightly in the little house. Gildaen crept to his favorite hiding place behind the woodpile. He was wild with curiosity. He wanted to know why these three looked as unhappy as they did.

"Tell us what has happened," asked Evon.

"A crowd was gathered in the square," said William Liddle. "They were listening to the king's herald reading a sentence on a criminal, a poacher—Hickory, by name," he said, pointing to the big man. "The sentence was banishment from the kingdom, on pain of death. Anyone giving aid or shelter to this Hickory would also be punished by death!"

There was silence in the room. Hickory had remained standing, clenching his fists.

"We must leave today," said Evon.

"No!" said Fara. "The herald was riding through every village reading the king's sentence. I'm afraid that wherever you go, Hickory will be recognized."

"Why, I see that both of you knew all along he was a hunted man!" the farmer said. "How could you let such a man into your house, Millie? I do not understand you!"

"Oh, Will, he is no criminal, though the king's sentence hangs over him. He and Evon and the rabbit Gildaen saved our lives, Fara's and mine."

"Rabbit?" said the farmer. "What are you talking of? How could a rabbit save your life?"

"Gildaen," called Evon. "No more hiding for you. Come out."

Although he was afraid of the farmer, Gildaen obeyed. He hopped to Evon's boot.

"I am here," he said.

"What's this?" cried the farmer in dismay, sinking back upon a stool. "A rabbit who speaks? Is this a den of wicked enchanters?"

"No, friend," Evon assured him. "There has been enchantment, but none of it is evil. I myself have been changed, I know not how, from my own shape, and the memory of who I am has gone from me. I have been able to give this rabbit the power to speak and to understand. Otherwise, he is no different from any rabbit of the field or wood."

"He ran to warn me, Will, when a band of thieving murderers came here looking for gold. These three have done us nothing but good." She hastily told him the story of Chough and his visit.

"It's too much for me," the farmer said. "Rabbits talking, men changed to crows. And this Hickory, you say, is no poacher."

"He has been unjustly accused," said Evon. "We are going back to Hearthfire to prove his innocence."

"But if he is seen, he'll be taken and put to death!" said Millicent Flann.

"He will hide near the castle. There must be a place you know of, Hickory, where you will be safe," Evon remarked.

"There is such a place," Hickory answered after a moment's thought, "a hut in the forest where hunters shelter at need."

"Then that is where you will stay," said Evon. "Gildaen and I will go to the castle.

"I am coming with you," Fara said.

"Why, Fara, what do you mean?" asked Millicent Flann. "You'll not leave us."

"Mother, I can help them," she pleaded. "I can introduce Evon to Uncle Walter. I can help him find out things. This is my chance to repay them for their kindness and all their help to us."

"I know not what to say," said her mother, looking from Fara's eager face into the eyes of Evon.

"Madam," said Evon. "The decision is yours. But she is right. She could help us at the court."

"I trust you," said Millicent Flann, "even with my most precious possession. Fara—if you will have it so—you may go."

"Oh, thank you, Mother!" said the girl.

"We should leave now," said Hickory. "We cannot walk too far or too fast in what is left of the day."

"You'll not walk at all," said the farmer. "My horses and wagon will take you. I'll use my second team for spring plowing. Your journey will be safer and the sooner over."

Millicent Flann's face beamed with gratitude. "Thank you, Will!" she said.

"A good gift brings blessings to the giver," said Evon. "So it will prove for you, William Liddle. May your sheep always bear fine, thick wool, your grass make sweet hay, and your apples stay ripe on the tree until they are picked!"

"I'll get my things together," said Fara.

"Wait, Fara," said Evon. "It seems best to me that we travel with a woman as your escort. Yes, Hickory, a woman. But do not look so grave. In a few moments I shall cease being Evon and become someone more suitable for this journey of ours. One last flourish, though, I must have!"

With these words he did a handspring, then a series of cartwheels across the floor. Finally he stood on his head.

"There," he said, righting himself. He was flushed from being upside down; his hair hung wildly around his face, and the light of mischief danced in his eyes. "I have had my fun. And now—farewell to Evon!"

Hardly had he finished speaking when he began to change. He grew taller and broader. The hair on his head grew longer and shaped itself into a neat bun. The face became rounder and older, a comfortable woman's face. This new personage resembled Millicent Flann enough to be reckoned a cousin of the same age. She was dressed in somber brown, a fringed shawl over her shoulders.

Gildaen was startled, but, after all, he had seen the owl change into the boy prince. The others stood rooted to the spot, amazed.

"Who would believe it?" whispered Millicent Flann.

"Not I, unless I had seen it with my own eyes," said Hickory.

"Master—or should I say 'Mistress' now?—what are you to be called?" asked Gildaen. "Evon won't do any more."

"You will have to find another name," said the former Evon in a voice they recognized. The same quiet authority they had counted on in Evon were in the voice. If it had changed at all, it was only to sound a shade fuller.

"How about 'Evonna,' then?" ventured Gildaen. "That will not sound unfamiliar to you or to us."

"Agreed. Henceforth I am Evonna."

Gildaen glanced at the farmer. He felt sorry for him.

Hardly had he had time to recover from meeting a talking rabbit when he was faced with Evon's transformation.

Now he roused himself and asked suspiciously, "Are
you not, in truth, a black magician?"

"No such thing, my friend. I have done no evil, nor
have evil spells or practices aided me," said Evonna reassuringly.

"You look like *her*," the farmer said, pointing to Millicent Flann.

"I suppose I had her in mind for someone Fara would
feel at home with," Evonna answered.

"To look at you, Sir Evon—I mean, Mistress Evonna—
fair takes my breath away," said Millicent Flann. "Why, it
is almost like meeting a new kinswoman."

"Good!" said Evonna. "I've been successful, then. But
now, friends, go and gather what you need. The afternoon
is going, and we must be on the road."

THE ROAD TO THE PALACE

HEIR POSSESSIONS AND PROVISIONS WERE quickly loaded into the wagon.

"You've given us much too much food," protested Hickory.

"Suppose you are delayed by bad weather?" Millicent Flann replied. "Who knows how long you may be on the road? I wish to know my child and my friends have what they need!"

Farmer Liddle gave the horses a pat. "If you have no

more need of these good beasts, send them home to me by some trusty driver, and I'll reward him for his labor."

"I will," promised Hickory.

"Good fortune go with you, friends," said Millicent Flann, trying to give them a farewell smile.

"Don't fear for us," said Evonna. "And remember, we will take good care of Fara."

Millicent Flann nodded and raised her hand to wave.

Hickory started the horses out of the farmyard. Fara turned and waved back until the little house and the two figures beside it vanished around a turn in the road. The horses stepped along briskly.

"A bit late for an outing!" whinnied Sall.

"Our driver is a man of sense, though, and gentle on the reins," Meg commented.

At this Evonna laughed. "The horses approve of you, Hickory!"

Their surroundings changed from forested valleys and patches of farmland drifted with snow to a land bare of trees. There were no houses in this scrubland. The road wound away into the distance across an icy wilderness where the wind had swept the snow into strange shapes. "Not a nice place at all," thought Gildaen with a shiver.

At dusk they were delighted to see ahead of them a circle of old pines off to one side of the road, trees that had weathered long years of storm and blast. They had not only survived, but grown tall and thick, though bent into strange shapes. They unhitched the horses in the shelter of the trees and kindled a fire. Evonna gave out oatcakes and cheese, and Fara helped Hickory to toast chunks of cold mutton over the fire. They fell to eating with a good appetite. Gildaen decided that oatcake was very good when eaten with carrots.

Gildaen sighed as he settled himself in the wagon next to Evonna. The pine trees reminded him of the firs growing in thick clumps on the hills above his home. Tender young grasses would soon come up near the thicket where his burrow was hidden, as well as snowdrops and violets. How delicious they were! He fell asleep imagining spring sunshine on fields of wild clover.

The next six days passed with a dreary sameness. They rose with the first light and drove the entire day, eating cold meals in the wagon while the horses rested and drank.

By the eighth day they saw signs that spring had come. The bare red switches of dogwood showed swelling buds, and the willows had already started to leaf.

"We're coming to the king's forest preserve," Hickory told them, "league upon league of wild forest."

Ahead of them the road suddenly took a decided turn for the better. It was level and well tended, very different from some of the stretches they had encountered. Giant oaks stood like sentinels on either side, their branches making an archway whose end could not be seen.

"There is the boundary," Hickory warned.

"How much farther, Hickory, to the palace itself?" Evonna asked.

"No more than half an hour's easy travel," he answered. He looked longingly at the road. "The trees go almost to the gates. Would that I might take you all the way!" His face was stony.

"Take us to the hiding place you told us of," said Evonna. "You must not risk being seen."

They journeyed on underneath the oaks, which kept their leaves through the winter, dark orange and brown. The roadway was majestic, but none of them could fully enjoy it, engrossed as they were in gazing down the road ahead watching for approaching horsemen. When they had been driving for some ten minutes, Hickory pulled the horses off the road to the right. He fastened the reins securely to the stout trunk of a guardian oak.

"We must leave the road here," he said.

"Shall we come with you?" Fara asked.

"That would be wise," Evonna said. "We do not know when we may need to find or fetch Hickory, and we should all be sure we can reach his hiding place."

Hickory led them into the forest, notching the trees as they went along.

"That may help you," he said.

"Won't these signs lead enemies to you?" Fara asked.

"None will question the marking of trees here. Hunters often do so to enable them to reach the road in safety again. Those who do not take such care have lost themselves forever, frightened witless, wandering until hunger and thirst finished them. I have hunted here with my father since I was a lad, but there are reaches of this wild wood even I have never explored."

They walked on a carpet of leaves, thick and soggy, and drifts of pine needles that gave a heady fragrance to the air. They skirted a bog and came at length to a clearing where wild grasses were sprouting. A crude hut of unsplit logs stood in its center. Hickory strode to the door and looked within.

"Hunters have not been here for a long time," he said.

"Are you sure you'll be safe here?" asked Fara.

"As safe as anywhere in this kingdom as long as Grimald has power," Hickory answered.

"Have you water nearby?" was Evonna's question.

"There is a stream behind the next hillock that winds through the forest. The water is clear and good. I shall want for nothing."

On their return Hickory took pains to point out the marks he had made and to show them how to avoid a bog. Gildaen had been enjoying the outing in the woods and the chance to stretch his legs, but now he began to wonder when he would see Hickory again. He had come to like and trust the big man as he never thought he could.

They made Hickory take the remaining food. Evonna wrapped the provisions in his blanket and gave them to him.

"Don't forget," he said, "that the Lord Royce may be able to help you if the Lord of the Bower has not disposed of him. Lord Royce is a wise man and a good one. I hope you can speak with him."

"I will seek him out," said Evonna.

"Farewell," said Hickory. "As for you, Gildaen," he said, bending down on one knee, "I promise you that no matter what is to be, your kindred are henceforth safe from me."

"I will miss you, Hickory," Gildaen said.

Hickory waved, then turned and disappeared into the woods.

The three companions were silent and low in spirit as they drove on toward the palace. During the many days that they had talked of coming to Hearthfire and dealing with Grimald, Gildaen had not really believed that the moment would arrive when talk must give way to action. He tried to imagine how they would manage; how could they get the best of a sorcerer?

Finally Fara broke the silence and asked, "What will you do at the palace, Evonna?"

"I hope your uncle will allow me to work in the kitchens," she replied.

"The kitchens!" Gildaen said. "But why?"

Evonna answered with some amusement. "Why not?

For one thing, a kitchen is always brimming with news and gossip; and for another, from there I may observe the young king and this Grimald without myself being observed by the Lord of the Bower's spies."

"The kitchens sound like an unfriendly place for a rabbit," said Gildaen. "I don't wish to be stuck in a pasty or minced for a stew!"

Evonna shook her head. "Gildaen, you have not come this far only to end as a rabbit pie, I promise you. But," she said, "I think you are right about one thing. We would be foolish to take you to the palace in your present form."

"You mean—I should be something else?" Gildaen asked.

"I have hesitated to transform any of you," said Evonna, "yet I think the risk is great if you enter the palace walls as you are."

Evonna spoke softly, but there was no mistaking the firmness in her voice. Gildaen looked at her for a long moment and saw in her eyes the same strength and kindliness that had made him first trust the boy prince in the castle garden near his home.

"All right," he said. "Change me!"

"What will you turn him into?" Fara asked anxiously.

"Something no one wishes to eat! Something useful in a kitchen. Do not bother to protest, Gildaen, that you are already useful. The cooks would find but one use for you!"

"Now, Gildaen, jump down beside the wagon," said Evonna as they halted once again.

Gildaen obeyed; he had the sensation that he was growing, yet at the same time shrinking. His ears were becoming smaller, and as if to make up for these vanishing ears, his trail stretched out behind him. His heart was beating fast as he landed on great soft paws that sheathed sharp claws. He looked down and saw that his legs and every part of his body that he could see was covered with tawny yellow fur. When he tried to speak, his voice came out as a hoarse roar.

The horses snorted and neighed wildly. Evonna held the reins tightly and spoke reassuringly to Meg and Sall. Only her steady hand and calm voice prevented them from bolting.

"He's a lion!" said Fara. "Oh, Gildaen, how frightening you are! I am afraid, even though I know that it's *you*."

Evonna shook her head. "How could I make such a mistake!" she said. "I meant to turn you into a cat, but only the household variety. This will never do. Sit down, please, and I will try once more."

Gildaen drew a deep breath and waited. Again he experienced the feeling of great change. The sensation of shrinking made him so dizzy that he closed his eyes.

"You did it!" said Fara, clapping her hands. "Gildaen, she's changed you into a cat, the handsomest I've ever seen."

Gildaen opened his eyes. Evonna was smiling down at him.

"I must admit I was worried," she said. "I wasn't sure you would turn out as I intended, even the second time, Gildaen. Practice does help, I see."

"Please don't practice on me any more than you must!" said Gildaen. "I feel very strange."

"You'll soon grow used to your new shape, Gildaen. And remember that your disguise will keep you safe. You are a hunter now, not one of the hunted. Come, jump up beside me."

With an easy, graceful leap Gildaen landed between Fara and Evonna.

"Now," said Evonna, "we are ready for the palace."

The road ahead of them widened, and high hedges of hawthorne replaced the oaks.

"We must be close!" said Fara.

The horses quickened the pace of their own accord. They knew that they were close to food and shelter. The road ran through a stone archway, flanked by guards on horseback. At the sight of them Gildaen sprang into his basket and Evonna closed the lid. The horsemen rode to meet them.

"Halt!" they called. "Your names and your errand?"

Evonna reined in the horses. "I am bringing this girl to her aunt and uncle," she said, imitating the motherly tones of the Widow Flann.

"And who may they be?" the older guard demanded.

"Walter Walloon is her uncle."

"Walter the Worrier, eh?" said the other guard. "Pass on, then."

"Not so hasty," said his companion. "Search the wagon."

The young soldier dismounted and climbed in from the back. He rummaged through their bundles.

"They've nothing of value, that's for certain," he said to the other guard. "Precious little of anything, I'd say."

"What have you in the basket?" asked the older guard.

"Only our cat," Evonna replied.

"Open the basket!" the guard commanded, and Fara lifted the lid. Gildaen cowered there, his eyes shut.

"All right," the guard snapped. "You may go on."

The lid was dropped again, to Gildaen's immense relief. Although he knew that he had nothing to fear in his guise as a cat, he could not help behaving like a rabbit.

"Do you always search visitors thus?" asked Evonna innocently.

The two guards exchanged an uneasy glance. "Of late,"

said the younger man, "many things have changed." He remounted his horse.

"Enough talk!" said his companion. "Drive through!"

The guards rode back to their posts, and Evonna drove the wagon through the stone archway. They had arrived.

THE KITCHENS

H!" SAID FARA AS THEY ENTERED THE COURT-
yard. Gildaen pushed his head gently against
the lid, which yielded to the pressure and
lifted slightly. He looked out and had a confusing impression of many buildings, a
hodgepodge.

The palace had originally been built as a simple hunting lodge in the reign of the young king's great-grand-
father, Justin I. The second Justin had desired to bring

more friends and retainers with him when he came hunting, and he had added rooms and levels at his whim and as the need for them arose, and so, too, had the present king's father. Thus, there were towers and courtyards and wings sprouting from the central building seemingly at random. There seemed to be no plan at all to the place.

"I shall never find my way about in there!" exclaimed Fara.

"It does look like a maze, doesn't it?" said Evonna. "But once we've been inside, we shall learn how to get where we wish to go."

Gildaen saw that even the materials of the palace were not of a kind. Some walls were of great blocks of stone, while the towers were built of brick.

"The kitchens are to be found at the rear, no doubt," said Evonna, maneuvering the horses. They passed wings devoted to the necessary palace crafts. Leather workers were plaiting harnesses, stitching boots and jerkins. Animal hides were hung on frames. Gildaen closed his eyes until they were well past these. He opened them again and watched a bowmaker testing the pull of a heavy bow, but they soon left him behind and came to row upon row of stables. Horses whinnied to Meg and Sall, who answered with eager neighs.

"At last," Sall said, "a place worth visiting!"

Grooms were leading horses to the grooming bars, where more than a dozen were being curried. Heavy-footed broad-backed draft horses were being unhitched from plows and from wagons used to haul logs from the forest. Separate from the others, the nobility of the stables were being groomed; these were the hunters, graceful of form, bred for speed and endurance in the chase. Gildaen admired these proud-looking beasts.

A blast of trumpets, spirited and gay, rang out, occa-
sioning a nervous stir of activity among the grooms. Evonna
halted the wagon near the plow horses and spoke to one
of the grooms.

"What is happening, good sir?" she inquired.

He stared at her before he answered. "You must be a
stranger here if you do not know that call. The king and
the Lord of the Bower will ride before dinner."

"Thank you, sir," she said. To Fara she whispered, "We
are in luck! We might have been here many days before
we caught a glimpse of them."

Fara leaned forward eagerly as the king's party approached. Gildaen had lowered his head when Evonna
spoke to the groom, but now, very cautiously, he lifted it
so that he might see both of these figures he had heard so
much about.

Justin IV walked beside a tall and somber lord. The
king's hunting suit was of soft green, and he wore no
sword but carried instead a braided leather crop. There
was no doubt in Gildaen's mind that this boy, only a few
years older than Fara, was a king. He walked with the
step of one who was used to walk first. Gildaen was
astonished to notice the resemblance between Justin and
Evonna's earlier guise as the prince. Gildaen wondered if
Fara noticed it as well.

The lord by Justin's side was dressed in shades of gray.
His short cloak was fastened with a silver brooch that
framed a black gem. He, too, had the look of one who
had never bowed to another's will. His face was lean and
bold. Gildaen shivered as he saw that the eyes in that face
were as dark, as stony, and as expressionless as the strange
gem he wore to buckle his cloak. The eyes revealed
nothing. His face was as closed to the gaze of an observer

as if it were concealed in a vizor. This, then, was Grimald, Lord of the Bower, he whom Hickory had good cause to hate. Before he heard him speak a word, Gildaen feared him. His instinct told him that this man was an enemy of the weak, a relentless, dangerous foe. He had great faith in Evonna, but he wondered if she could best such an enemy.

Evonna also was considering the Lord of the Bower with much interest, but Gildaen could see no fear in her measured gaze, and that helped to reassure him. The young king strode to his waiting horse, a chestnut stallion whose saddle was ornamented with gold tooling. The horse appeared nervous. He pawed the ground as the prince lightly mounted. Grimald rode a powerful gray with black mane and tail, harnessed in black and silver. As if by accident, the Lord of the Bower allowed his mount to brush against the king's. When the chestnut shied away, Justin gave him a cruel blow with his crop.

"Confound you, Bayard!" he said angrily. "I will cure you of this folly!" He struck the horse again. Bayard whinnied in pain and reared high in the air. Justin was an experienced rider and braced himself. He struck the horse a third time as he came down and urged him forward. He was off at a gallop, his courtiers striving to catch up with him. Again the trumpets rang out, and the hunters were gone.

"Horrible!" snorted Meg.

"Bayard was afraid," whinnied Sall. "The man in gray was at fault. I would shy from him myself!"

"That dreadful boy!" exploded Fara. "Did you see how ill he used his horse? He is not fit to be a ruler!"

"I am surprised, I confess," said Evonna. "Hickory told us that the young king was a good-hearted, kindly boy."

The grooms were talking together in low voices. The groom who had spoken to them earlier came over, shaking his head.

"Don't be judging our young master by what you saw, ma'am," he said. "I've been groom here since that boy was no more than a baby. A better horseman, for his years, I've never seen. He had no crop until this last year, nor did he need one. He had but to urge his beast with a touch or a word."

"Then why did he strike him today?" asked Fara, still indignant.

The groom's face darkened. "That is the doing of *him*, that man with the black heart who rode against Bayard." He almost spat the words. "The Lord of the Bower he's called," he said. "I would that he and his sneaking, skulking crew were back where they came from!"

"What have they done then," asked Evonna, "to deserve your dislike?"

"They're everywhere, those men of his, prying into every corner. They do his evil work, helpin' him put poison in the king's mind, so that he does not even trust his oldest friends."

"Friends like Hickory," said Evonna, watching the groom's face closely.

"Hickory!" he said, looking at them suspiciously. "Maybe I have said too much to you, strangers. Maybe you were sent for by Grimald. Well, I care not! Let your master know that Hace the groom is no coward." He turned on his heel and started to walk away.

"Wait!" said Evonna. "There is no need for you to leave us. We are friends of Hickory also."

The groom halted and surveyed them appraisingly. "If that's the truth, then where is Hickory now?"

"He is well," Evonna answered. "Through the winter he stayed at the home of this girl's mother. He longs to return here."

Hace's freckled face broke into a grin. "It's true then. You know him, and he's alive! The rumor was that Grimald's men followed him into the wild wood and did away with him."

"He's very much alive," said Evonna.

"Aye," said Hace, resuming his glum look, "but I'd not give two straws for his life if he were to come back now! If the Lord of the Bower so much as lays eyes on Hickory, he'll have him murdered."

"We hope to find some way to deal with the Lord of the Bower. May we count on your help?" Evonna asked.

"You can, and there's plenty of others who'd lend a hand if they thought they could get rid of him."

"We shall try, never fear. Now, will you guide us to the kitchens? Fara is waiting to see her aunt and uncle."

Hace obligingly walked alongside the wagon, directing them, pointing out features of the palace grounds. When they reached the door that led to the kitchens, Hace asked Fara. "Who's your uncle? What name shall I give?"

"His name is Walter Walloon. Tell him Fara is here."

"Walter's a decent one, he is," said Hace, "though he does fret himself too much, and others, too." He disappeared into the kitchens.

An appetizing aroma was wafted out to them before the door was closed again, a mingling of the aromas of meats, herbs, soups, and pasties baking.

"Umm," said Fara, closing her eyes. "I had forgotten that I was hungry!"

"Your uncle will be busy preparing dinner for the court."

The door burst open and a woman emerged, wiping her floury hands on her apron. She was followed closely by a tall man enveloped in a cook's apron that covered him from shoulders to knees.

"Fara!" cried the woman.

Fara jumped down from the wagon and embraced her, receiving a floury hug. "What is it, Fara?" asked the woman, gazing worriedly into her face. "Is your poor mother in trouble? Has she fallen ill?"

"Aunt Wilma," said Fara. "How glad I am to see you!"

"Perhaps I can explain," volunteered Evonna. They turned to her, eager and curious.

"Fara's mother is to be wed to her good neighbor, Farmer Liddle. A friend and I promised to bring Fara to you for a visit."

"Who are you?" said the man in the apron. "Your story makes little sense to me."

"My name is Evonna, and you are right, Walter Walloon, if you are he, there is much more to be told, but this is neither the time nor the place for the full tale. Is this all the welcome for us after our days of travel?" There was reproach in Evonna's calm voice.

"She is right, Walter!" burst out Fara's aunt. "Come in, both of you. We can talk later!" She threw an angry glance at her husband.

"Come in, yes, come in," echoed her husband sheepishly. "I am wrong to question you here," he said. He helped Evonna from the wagon. She carried the basket on her arm.

"What have you there?" he asked.

"Our cat, Gildaen," she replied.

"I hope he's a better hunter than our lazy stuff-guts here. The mice and rats plague me!"

Gildaen realized that he would have to meet other cats. He doubted that he could face one without giving away his fear.

Behind the kitchen door was a room as large as the great hall of the ruined castle where Chough's men had lived. This area was crowded with workers busy at the tables set up in every part of the chamber. The tables were heaped with various foodstuffs. Cooks were cutting out dough and shaping pasties; near them women were kneading bread dough into rolls and twists for table bread. Butchers were carving, chopping, stuffing, and seasoning a variety of meats and fowl. The entire back wall was a fireplace, with many separate cooking fires over which were suspended kettles and cauldrons. The spits were being tended by scullions whose task it was to see that the meat browned evenly without burning. Beside them were buckets of water to douse flare-ups in the coals caused by the dripping meat juices. Gildaen was happier to see the several tables given over to vegetables, which a small army of women was peeling, slicing, mincing, or dicing. Gildaen's stomach began to remind him that he had not eaten in some hours.

"Goodness!" said Fara, surveying the activity. "Is it dinnertime?"

"Not yet," replied her uncle, flurried by this question. "Oh dear, no! We still have time to finish our work. When the king returns from his ride, he will call for his meal, and I must have it ready for him!" He stopped before one of the bubbling cauldrons and motioned for a wooden spoon. He tasted the sauce, looked thoughtful, smacked his lips, and took another spoonful. He pulled a worn sheaf of papers from his apron pocket and leafed through them. "Pepper," he muttered, "grilled cumin, celery seed, mint, thyme, savory, safflower, toasted walnuts, honey, wine, vinegar, oil of walnut. Yes, more vinegar!" he said to the assistant.

"You," he called to a man half asleep by the hearth. "Stir that gallimaufry before it turns to glue!"

They crossed the length of the room and were almost at the opposite door when he dashed over to a table where cheeses were being set out.

"No, no, no!" he moaned in obvious distress. "Must I do everything myself? Can you not see that these must be arranged more delicately for the king's table? Cut them neatly into wedges—the tray looks as if you've broken the cheeses, or worse still, chewed off chunks!"

He was shaking his head as he rejoined them. "I cannot trust anyone to do as I wish. Everyone is against me! The king will send me away, or boil me in one of my own pots if his meal is not just as it should be. It is a wonder my hair is not all turned white!"

"Now, Walter," said his wife, giving his arm a pat, "you are too hard on yourself. Your dinner will be a feast, as it is every day. Only yesterday the king complimented you on your sauces."

"But that was yesterday!" he said with some exasperation. "This is another day. These careless fools will surely ruin me!" he exclaimed.

His wife took him by the arm and led him from the kitchen into one of the palace corridors. Guards in scarlet and gold livery stood at attention at both ends of the hall-way but took no notice of them. Wilma Walloon opened the door to a room not far from the kitchens, motioning Evonna and Fara to enter. They found themselves in a small sitting room looking out on an inner courtyard.

"Our bedchamber is in there, Fara," said her aunt, pointing toward the only other door in the room. "Are you and your friend weary?"

"Not too weary to talk to you, Aunt," answered Fara politely.

"Tell us your story then, child, as quickly as may be. We must be back at our work, for this is the busiest time of day for us."

"We came with a friend," said Fara. "He is hiding not far from here, Uncle. He is accused of a crime of which he is innocent. Evonna is here to help him, and I will give her what aid I can."

"What is this friend's name?" asked Walter Walloon in a voice that quavered.

"His name," said Evonna firmly, "is Hickory."

"He is alive, then!" responded Wilma Walloon, clasping her hands.

"Does anyone here know that you are his friends?" questioned Walter Walloon.

"We told the groom, Hace, who brought us to you," said Fara.

"Oh, shades of pepper and fennel, oh, my blackest cook pots, what is to become of us?" Walter Walloon moaned, pacing up and down the chamber. "Ill fortune follows me wherever I go!"

"We will not endanger you, or anyone else here at the palace," said Evonna coldly.

"If you are afraid, Uncle, we will not stay here," Fara said in a low voice.

"Alack the day, Fara!" he said, coming to stand before her. "I am a man who would like to be cheerful and hopeful, but it is not in my disposition, if you understand me. I don't want you to go! And I am an eel-and-bacon idiot to berate you so. *Stay*," he said, stretching out his hand to her, "and your aunt and I will try to help you, though how I cannot say!"

Fara took her uncle's offered hand. "Thank you, Uncle

Walter," she said, smiling at him for the first time. "I promise to be careful. We'll not cause you more trouble."

"Think no more of it, child," said Wilma Walloon, embracing her niece again. "Hickory is a fine man, and he has many friends here. And you, Mistress Evonna," she said, turning to her, "we owe you much for bringing our Fara to us on so long a journey. How may we show our thanks?"

"For the present, your husband can give me a job in the kitchens, if he will," said Evonna.

Walter Walloon looked her up and down. "What can you do?" he asked critically.

"I shall help in any way you wish, but I have knowledge of herbcraft, and I shall not disappoint you as a cook."

"That's very well to say," responded Walter Walloon, "but I need someone I can trust to assist me in making up the courses for the king's table. How do I know that you can do what you say you can?"

"You have only to try me," replied Evonna.

"I shall!" he cried, dashing from the room. Fara looked after him in astonishment. Her aunt saw the expression on her face and said, "Fara, you've forgotten your uncle has little ways which take getting used to, but believe me, both of you, he is the kindest soul who ever drew breath. He pretends, sometimes, to be angry, yet never has an unkind deed followed his words."

"I know, Aunt Wilma."

Before she had time to say more, Walter Walloon was back with a tray containing a covered bowl, two spoons, and a shaker. He set down the tray and uncovered the bowl. An inviting aroma rose from the contents, which appeared to be a stew. He gave one spoon to Fara and the other to Evonna and motioned to them to eat.

"How is it?" he asked eagerly.

A smile came to Fara's face. "Delicious!" she said, taking another spoonful.

"What do you think, Mistress Evonna?" he asked.

"It lacks marjoram," she said reflectively. "Should it not also have a hint of caraway? I detect none."

"Marvelous!" cried Walter Walloon, clapping his hands and dancing a little jig around the room. "At last! Someone with a palate as delicate as my own. You are as good as your word! If you are not too weary, come and help me with the evening's meal. There are a thousand details I must attend to. Marjoram, of a certainty!" he exulted, taking the shaker and shaking a little of that herb into their stew. "And caraway! I hadn't thought of it myself. Our meals will be the finest the king has ever tasted!" Shaker in hand, he ran from the room once more.

The others burst into laughter. For the first time since he had been carried into the palace, Gildaen was at ease. He had wondered for a while whether Fara's uncle would throw them out.

When they recovered from their laughter, which seized them like a fit after the soberness of the earlier conversation, Wilma Walloon said, "I am grateful to you, Mistress Evonna, for lightening my husband's mood. He frets and worries over each dish! I hope you can make his days easier. I am content to keep the scullery in good hand and perform whatever tasks he sets for me, but I am no cook."

Evonna put down her spoon. "This stew is excellent. I shall do my best for him," and she stood up.

"Are you going now, Evonna?" Fara asked.

"I think your uncle would welcome my presence in the kitchen. You must try to rest, Fara."

Fara yawned. "I am tired," she confessed.

"Why, to be certain you are, love," said her aunt. "I'll make you up a pallet on the floor, and another for Mistress Evonna, until we can find better quarters."

She took blankets from a wooden chest, as well as feather comforters, and arranged two sleeping places.

"Rest well," called Evonna, following Wilma Walloon from the chamber.

Gildaen was glad to leave the basket and stretch.

"You really are beautiful, Gildaen," Fara remarked admiringly. "That soft gray fur and your green eyes are most unusual. I've seen barn and village cats, but never a one like you! Evonna must have fashioned you after a royal cat."

Gildaen padded about the room, poking his nose into every corner.

"I hope," he said, his inspection complete, "the other cats will not suspect that in my heart I am a rabbit!"

"You must try to think like a cat, Gildaen," Fara said with a laugh.

"How *does* a cat think? Or act, for that matter?" he answered reproachfully. "I've had nothing to do with them, thank goodness, before this."

"For one thing, they walk quietly and gracefully. You do that very well."

"It seems to come naturally."

"Also, cats chase birds."

"I could never do that!" Gildaen said indignantly.

"Then you must at least pretend. Also, you must try to kill mice and rats."

"Never!"

"But, Gildaen, you needn't ever really catch one. You have only to pretend."

"I am hungry right now," he said. "But I don't know

what I am hungry for. The idea of eating a bird or rat makes me sick, but I don't believe I want vegetables either. I am puzzled, and my stomach is, too!"

The door opened again, and Evonna returned, carrying a large bowl. She set it down before Gildaen.

"Here you are," she said. "A bowl of fresh milk from the kitchen."

"Just the thing!" exclaimed Gildaen. He lapped up the entire bowl of milk hungrily as they watched.

"That was thoughtful of you, Evonna," he said when he had finished and licked his chin. "I was afraid that I might starve to death before I found something I could eat."

"Starve next door to the royal kitchens? I doubt it! We will see to it you do not go hungry," said Evonna, turning to leave.

"Must you go back?" Fara asked sleepily.

"Yes. There is still much to be done. I have been thinking about Grimald, and his face is somehow familiar to me, like the face of one in a dream. I have seen him before; where, I cannot remember. He has gained much power over Justin, and he is extending his sway. We must find out all we can about him. Gildaen, you will be able to make your way unnoticed throughout the palace. To-morrow you must begin to watch and to listen for us, but for tonight, sleep, both of you!"

Gildaen was pleasantly full. He decided that being a cat might be an interesting experience. Exploring the palace would be an adventure in itself. He curled up next to Fara. He was purring contentedly before he fell into the best sleep he had enjoyed since they left the Flann farm.

THE COUNCIL OF CATS

 HEN GILDAEN AWOKE FOR THE SECOND TIME, the room was dark. He found, however, that he could see very well, better than he had ever seen before at night. Earlier he had awakened briefly when Evonna and the Walloons returned and went quietly to their sleeping places. Now he was fully awake, restless, eager to be up and exploring. The idea of wandering about the palace in the dead of night, which ordinarily would have filled him with dread, intrigued him. He wondered idly if this inclination was common to cats. The darkness had never before been inviting! Noiselessly he rose and went to the door, which was shut tight, and so he padded across to the window that faced the courtyard. He found it open, just enough for him to jump up lightly and squeeze through. He heard something, a murmur of whispers that he could not quite make out. In the darkness he could distinguish raised flower beds, covered with straw for the winter. From the straw came a faint rustling and the whispers that had caught his attention. He leaped onto the stones of the yard and crept stealthily closer. With his excellent eyesight he saw that there were cats in the straw, and he froze where he crouched. Every instinct cried out to him to run, to escape, before he was discovered. He had to remind himself that in the eyes of these cats he was one of their kind. He decided to risk getting closer so that he could listen to their conversation. Evonna had said that his job was to garner information, and surely the cats were a good source of news. They moved at will about the palace, observed everything, and were themselves unobserved. He crept to the edge of the straw in time to hear a cat say, "You have it soft and easy, Mignon, lolling on your cushion in the king's chambers! It's easy for you to talk!"

"I sssuppose I am fortunate, Scudder," purred a soft voice in reply. "Yet I misss having women in the royal chambers! The court was much more graciousss when the young king's mother was alive."

"Don't talk about those days!" growled a rough voice. "We have to live with things as they are now. It's hard enough without your reminding us of good times."

"But, Dauber, I thought you liked being a ssstable cat," the cat called Mignon said reproachfully. "You have al-

ways enjoyed the sssport the mice give you, and the chance
to challenge the dogs from time to time."

"Right, I do. But things are not what they were since
the Lord of the Bower came with his own grooms. One of
them aimed a kick at me last week. I paid him back in
kind. He'll not use that leg to kick with for many a day!"

"That riff-raff," sniffed Mignon scornfully. "One of
them ssstepped on my tail! Sssuch clumsiness! You have
only to contend with his men, but I must sssee *that man*
himself. He hardly letsss King Justin out of his sssight."

There was a general growl of agreement.

"Only today," reported Dauber, "he upset Bayard so
that the king whipped him. A fine state of affairs when the
king doesn't know what's at fault with his own horse!"

"Did you see the newcomer?" asked the cat called
Scudder.

"What newcomer?" asked Dauber, an edge of disap-
proval in his tone.

"The one with gray fur—looks a bit like you, Mignon.
He came in a basket with the woman and girl who drove
up in a wagon."

"Didn't see him," Dauber said.

"Never mind that, for now," said Mignon impatiently.
"I have a sssecret to tell you! I've been *ssso dissstresssed* I
hardly know what to do. Come clossser," she said, dropping
her voice lower still. Gildaen took one furtive step nearer.

"Wait!" warned Dauber. "I heard something!" He
sprang out of the straw directly into Gildaen's path.

Gildaen had never imagined that he would be able to
stand as calmly as he did. The cat facing him was enormous, yellow-furred with golden glints in his eyes. Bits of
fur were missing from his coat. His ears and face were
scarred by battle. Gildaen realized that this was a tomcat

who spent his life in combat, an experienced battler who feared no one. He gazed at Gildaen with suspicion, the fur rising on his back. "Who in the world might you be?" he questioned with an ugly growl.

"Gildaen is my name, sir," he responded instinctively, aware that if he were in his true shape, this cat would finish him off with one swipe of a powerful paw.

"Gildaen, eh? You the newcomer?"

"Yes. I heard voices and I hoped to meet some of the palace cats." This was not strictly the truth, to be sure, Gildaen thought, but he hoped the explanation would help him in his uncomfortable situation.

"Dauber," called Mignon with authority, "let him come up!"

"Let's have a look at him," said Scudder.

Dauber moved aside, and Gildaen jumped into the midst of the cats, who eyed him with great interest.

"He don't look right to me. I don't know why," said Dauber, following him.

"Nonsssense," scolded Mignon. "He *does* resemble me, Scudder, as you said, and all our family are of gentle birth and breeding. Tell me, ssstranger," she said softly, in an encouraging way, "where do you come from? What do you call yourself?"

"Gildaen, madam," he answered as politely as he could, "is my name, and I come from long journeying."

"Yes, we know you have been traveling. Our family has always had great travelers, but where were you born? You look well cared for and gently bred. Surely your first master was a nobleman?"

Gildaen had a happy thought. "Yes, madam," he said, bowing his head to her, "my master was the Prince Evon."

"You see!" she said triumphantly. "I knew it! Gildaen,

you must come and stay with me, in the young king's chambers. He will welcome another handsome cat, and you shall have a braided collar like mine and dainties from the king's own table."

"I give you my heartfelt thanks, madam, but I must spend most of my time with my young mistress."

"Sssuch good manners!" commented Mignon. "Breeding does tell, as I have always maintained."

"I hope I may come and visit with this company again?" Gildaen asked respectfully.

"We have many meeting places," said Scudder. "We change off and go wherever we think it will be quiet and cozy."

"If you don't mind my asking, are the four of you special friends? Is that why you come together?" Gildaen questioned.

The others meowed with amusement. Dauber glowered at him. "Do we look as if we would choose each other as friends?" he growled. "Not much brain in this branch of your family," he said to Mignon.

Gildaen now saw that the four cats were indeed very different, one from another. Mignon was a heavy, dignified-appearing cat whose gray fur was perfectly groomed. A collar of intricately braided red and gold leather was fastened about her neck. Dauber looked as if no part of his fur had ever gone in the same direction as any other part. Scudder was a black cat with white forepaws and a white diamond of fur on his chest. The other cat, whose coat was a gingery orange color, had been observing Gildaen silently. Now he said pleasantly, "Rustrim's the name, friend. We are the palace council, we four. We make the laws and keep the peace for the cats who live in the palace and on the grounds."

"Are there many?"

"Dozens," he said. "We'd never have any peace or order without the council. The four of us get together from time to time to decide what needs to be talked over. Mignon here speaks for the cats who live as pets of the nobles or the palace workers. The stable cats and those who live in the workshops chose Dauber as their leader. He can out-claw and out-jaw any cat in the palace. Scudder's mates live in the granaries and storehouses where the rats are the most plaguing. They're tough and quick! And I'm in charge of the kitchen and the scullery, as well as the royal pantries, a big job I can tell you. I saw you and your folks in the kitchens earlier today. Welcome to the palace!"

Gildaen purred his thanks. "May I stay here with you?" he asked. "It's a long while since I've been with other cats." "That," he thought to himself, "is surely true!"

"Why not?" said Scudder. "Our secrets are not kept from the other cats. Most of them are too lazy or too busy with their own affairs to bother to come to our meetings."

"Yes, and now let us go back to our business," said Mignon. "Before Gildaen joined us, I was about to tell you sssomething of the greatest urgency. This evening as I was dozing in the king's antechamber, I overheard a conversation. I was *ssso* upsset I could ssscarcely control myself, but I wanted to hear what was sssaid, and I continued to lie there with my eyes closed, pretending to sssleep. The Lord of the Bower and one of his henchmen were talking in low voices. The man called Growze said that he would find some way to kill the king sssoon, and Grimald replied, 'It must look like an accident.' His henchmen asked, 'What about poison, as usual?' whereupon the Lord of the Bower said, 'Fool! I told you it must look like an accident. Poisoning would arouse suspicion. No one must be able to lay the blame on me!' The two of them sat arguing for a while, until I felt I must jump up and ssscratch their eyes out! Finally, the Lord of the Bower said, 'I have the way. We will go boar hunting.' Growze had a gleam of evil glee in his eye and said, 'You mean old Crookjaw? He's a killer, that boar; he's gored the best of the hunting dogs when they tread too close behind him.' His master said, 'Exactly. We will find the boar and mislead the king's men away from the spot, leaving the king to face him alone. Crookjaw will take care of him for us!' Then he smiled his horrid smile, while his underling congratulated him on the plan."

Gildaen was horrified. How could they possibly thwart such a plot? Hickory could not help them. If their plot succeeded, Hickory would always be an outlaw, and evil days would come to the kingdom, to men and animals alike!

Dauber reacted first. "I'll leap onto his neck! I'll claw him into a thousand pieces of wickedness!"

"Hold on," said Scudder, calm and unmoved. "That won't work. The Lord of the Bower has eyes in the back of his head, I'd swear, and I've heard he has magical powers that would frizzle your whiskers."

"Scudder's right; you'd never be able to get at him."

Gildaen and the members of the council sat concentrating on the problem. Dauber's tail was lashing the straw furiously.

Gildaen asked, "When did they say they would have the boar hunt?"

"I don't know," wailed Mignon. "Anytime in the next few days."

"We must keep the king from going hunting!" Gildaen said.

"Good enough," said Rustrim, "but how do we manage that?"

"Maybe he will not be inclined to hunt?" suggested Mignon.

"Stuff-and-nonsense! He hunts almost every day he is here," said Dauber.

"What if he were to fall sick?" asked Gildaen.

"Sick?" said Scudder. "Why should he be sick? He's as fit as a cat in a full larder."

"We must make him sick somehow," insisted Gildaen.

"But we don't want to hurt him!" chided Mignon.

"We don't wish him killed either," Gildaen reminded her grimly.

"Do you have a plan, Gildaen?" asked Rustrim.

"My little mistress and the woman Evonna will be working in the kitchens. Suppose that some potent herb were placed in the king's food?"

"He would taste it and send the dish back. Walter Walloon would be blamed," said Rustrim. "He is good to the kitchen cats."

"He would be blamed if the king can taste the herb. It must be something with a subtle flavor that will work after the king has left the table."

"Your idea sounds crazy to me," said Dauber. "Even if it works, the king will go hunting again in a few days."

"But that would give us more time to think of something else," argued Scudder. "I am in favor of Gildaen's plan. Who else votes yes?"

Mignon and Rustrim raised their tails in agreement.

"If you others are willing, I will agree too," grumbled Dauber, "though I don't know how he means to carry it out."

"Leave it to me," Gildaen said, more confidently than

he felt. "I will see to it!" His brain was racing ahead, trying to imagine what Evonna would say to this news. If anyone could accomplish his plan, it was Evonna. In the meantime, he could hardly wait to get back to her. Soon it would be daybreak, and the humans who worked in the kitchens would be at work. He began to fidget. The tip of his recently acquired tail twitched. He realized that a cat must take care not to give away his thoughts with a careless motion of his tail.

"Gildaen, we are grateful to you for undertaking this venture," said Mignon in her pompous way. "When will you visit me to tell me more?"

"Perhaps later this morning, madam," he replied.

"I shall expect you," she said, nodding. "Do you know the sign?"

"The sign?" he asked, puzzled.

"The pass signal so our scouts will allow you to pass freely from one part of the palace to another. Without it, you would have to fight your way from place to place."

"I should learn it, in that case!"

"Wave your tail, first right, then left, three times."

"The hour is late! I declare this meeting at an end," said Scudder. In the blink of an eye, Gildaen found himself alone. The other cats had leaped out of the straw and were gone, each to his secret place of entry in the courtyard. Roosters in the palace barns were crowing, trying to outdo each other. Gildaen wondered how Chanticleer liked his new roost in Farmer Liddle's barn. He retraced his steps, feeling more anxious the more he thought over their difficulties. How could they keep the Lord of the Bower from accomplishing his purpose? Everything was in his favor. The young king trusted him and seemed completely under his influence. Grimald's men would stop at nothing to help him seize control of the throne, and worst of all, he was a sorcerer! Even so, they had to find a way to stop him.

When he squeezed through the window again, he found Evonna and Fara talking.

"There you are, Gildaen!" said Fara, relieved. "We had no idea where you were."

"I'm sorry to have caused you uneasiness," Gildaen replied, "but I have found out something we should discuss right away."

"About Hickory?" asked Fara.

"Listen!" said Gildaen, and proceeded to tell them the tale Mignon had related.

"How dreadful!" cried Fara. "Whatever is to be done?"

Diffidently, Gildaen told them his idea for delaying the plot.

"A worthy plan," said Evonna. "I myself will see to it that the king will not feel like hunting today."

"Won't my uncle be blamed?" asked Fara. "I promised him we would cause him no further trouble."

"No, Fara," Evonna reassured her. "I shall make sure that no one suspects the food as the cause. I intend to use the same stramony on Justin that I used when I wished you to have a good rest during your sickness. The king will feel the need for sleep, nothing more. But that will not keep him from the boar after today! Come along with us, Gildaen. Perhaps you will learn more that can be of use to us."

In the kitchens the activity and commotion were as intense as they had been the previous afternoon. Walter Walloon interrupted his supervision of the breakfast preparations to greet them and hurry Evonna to the table where the roasts and ragouts were already being prepared

for the noonday meal. Fara's aunt said, "We will break
our fast later, Fara dear, after the court has eaten. Then
we have an hour's leisure."

Gildaen saw a familiar face across the room, that of
Rustrim, who gave him a friendly welcome. Gildaen
joined him at a bowl of fresh warm milk, which he
hungrily helped to finish. "We eat well in this kitchen,"
confided Rustrim, "and the mice are plentiful!" That
comment made Gildaen pause in licking his whiskers
clean. He knew very well that he could never catch a
mouse, even if he wished to do so. He hoped he would
not be put in the position of having to chase one!

"What is our job in the kitchens, aside from catching
mice and rats?" Gildaen asked.

"Why, the cooks like to have us around. Gives them the
feeling that the mice will not be scampering beneath their
feet—and there are some bold ones, let me tell you! You
should hear the yowl from the women when they sight
one!"

"We have no other work, then?"

"Scavenging the kitchens, licking up the crumbs and
tidbits the cooks let fall. Other than that, our time is our
own."

"A nice arrangement, I should say!"

"And so should I. Remember, though, that days are
leaner once the king goes back to Castelmaine. We have
slack time here, but the weather is good and we can go
back to stalking out of doors."

Gildaen was having trouble remembering whose side
he was on. He had always thought of cats as fiendish murderers, yet he could appreciate that from a cat's point of
view hunting came naturally, especially when one needed
to fill an empty belly.

Rustrim finished grooming his fur, gave a sigh and a yawn, and stretched himself fore and aft. He looked very much as if he were getting ready to take a nap.

"When should I visit Mignon?" Gildaen asked hurriedly.

"Now, if you like," said Rustrim obligingly. "I will show you the way before I settle back for a snooze beside the fire. I can open an eye now and again to see any morsels that drop from the roasts as they turn."

Gildaen followed the ginger cat as he wove in and out among the legs of the workers putting the final touches on the breakfast. One woman chirruped to Rustrim as he went by and tossed him a bit of bacon, which he neatly caught and ate without slowing his pace. "No wonder he looks so content," Gildaen thought. "If he ate like that the year through, he would be too fat to catch anything for himself."

They waited beside one of the doors until a servingman with a full tray opened it and they could go through to the dining hall on the other side. Here, too, a huge hearth, built of enormous stones, blazed with a fire that took the chill from the high-ceilinged chamber. King Justin's table was close to the fire, but far enough away so that the king's party would not be uncomfortably hot. The courtiers at the other tables were already seated when the king and his attendants entered and sat down. When the king lifted his goblet, the members of the court lifted theirs in salute and the meal began. The hall rang with the sounds of hungry people laughing and talking and filling themselves noisily with as much food as they could stuff in. Gildaen remembered what Mignon had said about the lack of the queen's influence on the court. He noticed that there were no women in the room.

"Where are the ladies?" he murmured to Rustrim.

"Abed and asleep, or gazing at themselves in their look-ing glasses, choosing a becoming robe, something of the sort," he replied. "They will be down in a while."

Gildaen suddenly noticed to his distress that there were a number of dogs in the room, five or six of them sitting close to the king's table.

"Look!" he whispered. His whiskers tingled.

"Pay them no heed, Gildaen," the other cat said casually. "They are the king's favorite hunting dogs. Theirs is the privilege of sitting near him when he dines. After each course they get the table scraps and bones."

"Won't they attack us?"

"Wouldn't think of it! First of all, they have good man-ners—better than most of these nobles who are bolting their food like swine!—and would not cause a commotion in the dining hall. Here we ignore one another. We have a kind of truce within the palace. And don't forget, Gil-daen," he added, "no hound wishes to chance having his eyes scratched out!"

They passed close to the king's table. The dogs lifted their heads and watched them pad by, but made no move of any kind toward them. Gildaen had the chance to see King Justin at close range. Again he was struck by the resemblance between the king and the boy prince Evon. This boy, though he had the same noble features and firmness of movement, wore a sullen look on his face, as if it were clouded by thoughts that did not be-long there. At his right sat Grimald, who was speaking to him in low, confidential tones. Four others at the table were dressed in the gray and black livery of the Lord of the Bower, and from Mignon's description Gildaen recog-nized one of them as Growze. The remaining lords at the table ate quietly, saying little or nothing.

Gildaen looked particularly at an elderly gentleman clad in blue from whose shoulders hung a gold medallion. His air of quiet authority and poise evoked Gildaen's interest.

"Who is that nobleman in blue?" he asked Rustrim.

"That one is the Lord Royce, an old and faithful servant of the late king. He used to be the king's chief counselor. A just man, and kind, whom the present king often turned to for good advice. Nowadays the king hardly speaks a word to him. The Lord of the Bower would gladly be rid of him if he could do it without suspicion. Mind you, if he succeeds in killing the king, you may be sure that he will dispose of Lord Royce speedily."

Gildaen had liked the man's face at once. This was the nobleman who, Hickory had believed, might help them!

"Where does he live?" he inquired, trying to seem casual in his questioning.

"His apartments are somewhere close to the king's, or so at least they were. Mignon will know better than I. She knows everything that goes on up there. Hurry along, Gildaen. I want my nap."

They trotted past the courtiers, who showed signs of slowing in their single-minded devotion to the meal. The servingmen were clearing some of the tables. Gildaen followed Rustrim through the open doorway into a broad hall that led to a wide stairway of polished stone. They pattered up the stairs until they reached the second level of the palace. Gildaen admired the rich tapestries and wall hangings. A cat was curled at the top of the stairs. He opened his eyes and observed them. Rustrim gave the signal, Gildaen repeated it, and the cat closed his eyes again. "He is the warden of the stair," Rustrim explained. "Now that he's seen you with me and you have given the signal, you will have no trouble going back down."

They turned into another spacious corridor, turned again, and came to stout doors emblazoned with the king's seal. The doors were open, and Gildaen looked into a spacious chamber handsomely furnished. Housemaids were dusting and sweeping, while two were making up the royal bed with its bed curtains of gilt and scarlet. Beside the bed on a silken cushion sat Mignon, grooming herself. Gildaen was struck again by the natural desire for cleanliness and good appearance that cats seemed to possess. He himself had felt the desire to make his fur smooth and lick his paws free of every trace of dirt. Only Dauber the stable cat had no concern about his looks.

Mignon glanced up and saw them. "Gildaen," she meowed. "Do come in!"

Rustrim said, "Good-bye, for now!" and without further ceremony he turned tail and hurried away.

Gildaen entered the royal bedroom somewhat timidly. He had never been in such a richly furnished room.

"Alas!" Mignon sighed as he sat down beside her. "What is to become of us when Grimald rules?"

He wondered how much to confide in her. He chose his words carefully. "King Justin will not hunt today."

"How can you be sure, Gildaen?"

"The woman Evonna will drug his food. He will be weary and fall into a deep sleep."

"How did she know that she should give him the drug?"

He took a deep breath and blurted out, "Because I told her of Grimald's plot."

"You *told* her? What do you mean?" she asked. "Can you speak to humans, then?" She shrank away from him.

"Don't be alarmed, please! I cannot tell you the whole tale now, but I am able to talk with Evonna and young Fara. Evonna has come here especially to bring about the downfall of Grimald."

"Dear me!" said Mignon. Her tail moved back and forth in an agitated way. "I hardly know what to say."

"*You* must help us to stop Grimald. I have told Evonna what an important position you hold here, and I know she counts on your assistance," said Gildaen, deciding that flattery might accomplish what truth could not.

A flicker of satisfaction appeared in her eyes. She purred ever so slightly in response to Gildaen's words.

"You speak like a true courtier, Gildaen. You must certainly be a relative of mine," she said. "Strange though your tale is, I will do what I can for this Evonna person. What help do you wish?"

Gildaen was much relieved. If Mignon had been too frightened to listen or to agree, the council of cats would have made his life in the palace impossible.

"I think," he said, "that Evonna should speak with the Lord Royce. Do you know where his sleeping quarters are?"

"They were once a few doors away. But now Grimald has those apartments." She fairly spat when she uttered the hated name. "The Lord Royce has been moved far down to the end of the hall of nobles. He has fallen on evil days, like many another."

"Will you show me the way?" he asked.

With languid dignity she left her cushion. They had no sooner reached the corridor when they heard the sound of footsteps. Toward them came the young king and the Lord of the Bower, trailed by several of his henchmen. King Justin was yawning and shaking his head as if to clear it.

"The hunt, sire," said the Lord of the Bower with a shade of impatience. "All is in readiness below."

"I will not hunt today," said the king, rubbing his eyes with both hands.

"The horses are saddled, and the court awaits your pleasure. Surely on so fine a day you will not miss the chance to be rid of Crookjaw?" Grimald said coaxingly.

"I cannot go, believe me," said Justin. "I am seized by such a desire to sleep that I can do nothing. Perhaps in an hour or two. I shall call for you when I have slept." He yawned again. "Lead the hunt yourself, if you care to, but I must leave you now." He clapped his hands, and the housemaids scurried away, leaving only the king's valet. The king motioned and the valet closed the doors, leaving the lords in the corridor. Gildaen thought that the Lord of the Bower's look would burn through the closed doors, so angry was the glance he turned on them. Then his face relaxed. "Tomorrow is another day," he said to Growze. "Tomorrow this young sluggard king will hunt, though he sleep this day away." They turned and went back the way they had come.

"Gildaen!" said Mignon, scarcely able to contain her excitement. "Your idea worked! The king is sssafe!"

"Only for today," Gildaen replied gloomily. "Something more must be done. Come, show me Lord Royce's chambers."

"Yes indeed, Gildaen." She hurried off, and he followed close behind. He thought he detected a new respect for him in her voice and manner.

CROOKJAW

N THE DOORWAY OF THE LITTLE HUT, HICKORY sat eating a meager noonday meal. The day was bright with spring sunshine. New grass in the clearing around the hut was a vigorous and vivid green. Everywhere spring had come in real strength after the dreary last weeks, when winter had held on with a stubborn grip. With a woodsman's eye he had noted the return of the brightly hued birds who had been wintering far to the south. Now the forest was noisy with their songs. Around the trunks of the ancient oaks the first violets clustered, yet none of these sights and sounds could gladden him. He thought about his friends: Were they safe? Had they been able to find Fara's kinsmen? Two days had gone by since he had said farewell to them by the side of the road.

He heard a swishing in the grass, and then Gildaen was there, sitting at his feet. He jumped up in his surprise and pleasure. "Gildaen!" he said.

"Sit down again, Hickory, please do sit down. When you stand up like that, you are so tall that I cannot talk to you without straining my neck!"

Hickory did as Gildaen bade him. "I never thought my heart would be gladdened by the sight of a rabbit I was not hunting," he said, smiling his broad smile at Gildaen.

"For my part," Gildaen replied, "I never thought I would willingly come and sit before a hunter!"

"Gildaen, are the others safe and well?" he asked.

"Quite well, thank you. Evonna sent me with news. First, I should tell you that she has disguised me as a cat. Yes, a cat!" he said, seeing Hickory's astonishment. "I know that sounds unsuitable, but the part has been easier to play than I would have guessed. She changed me back to my own shape so that I might reach you as quickly as possible, but she says that when I reach the palace grounds, I shall become a cat again, and I hope she is right! There are too many other cats about for me to be safe as myself."

"I cannot get used to this form changing, Gildaen. I think I would have trouble being anyone but myself," said Hickory.

"At this moment, Hickory, your own face would land you in the dungeons—or worse!—should it be seen in the palace. Nothing has changed since you were banished except that the Lord of the Bower controls your young master more and more."

Hickory slapped his knee. "That bird of carrion! He still hangs on the king like a shadow, then."

"Far worse. Listen to what I have to tell you before you speak, Hickory. There is no time to be lost."

Gildaen recounted the story he had heard from Mignon at the council of cats. Hickory's mouth settled in a hard line, but he did not interrupt. Gildaen explained to him the manner in which they had kept Grimald from carrying out his plan the previous day.

"The young king slept almost the entire day yesterday. He was confused and somewhat dull when he awoke. The Lord of the Bower may suspect something, but he doesn't know quite what. He is not used to having his plans thwarted! No suspicion fell on Walter Walloon or Evonna."

"How did she accomplish it?"

"She added a few drops of the stramony root to the king's breakfast, only enough to do what was necessary. But listen—there is more. I took her to a secret conference with Lord Royce."

"That good man! I am glad the Lord of the Bower has not yet undone him."

"He will surely do so once the king is dead! Even I can see that Grimald hates him. Evonna and Lord Royce were closeted together for more than an hour. I stood guard, or, I should say, sat guard, outside his door, pretending to be asleep, but watching for Grimald's spies. When Evonna came out, the old lord bowed to her. His face had a hopeful look, I thought, but Evonna was deep in thought as we walked back to our sleeping quarters. Finally, she told me that they had decided that you must help us. Do you know where the boar Crookjaw has his lair?"

"Crookjaw is a crafty one! He does not rest long in any place but wanders from one lair to another. For once, though, Gildaen, we are in luck. Yesterday while I was sleeping, I heard something that brought me up at once, a crashing and a stamping. I looked out and saw Crookjaw himself step into the clearing. I have not laid eyes on the brute for more than a year, but there is no mistaking him. No hunting dog can bring him down, and no hunter has had better luck. I know well, for I have tried myself to spear him more than once. He rooted among the oaks, raised his head, and listened. Then he went off again to the west. There is a lair of his not too far from here in that direction, and it is my guess, Gildaen, that he is there now."

"Good! Evonna says that I must talk with him."

"Talk with him! Talk to a killer like that? He'll gore you and trample you and have you for breakfast."

"He must catch me first, Hickory," Gildaen answered boldly, though he did not care for Hickory's description of what was in store for him. "You did not hear me come today until I was beside you, and I can be much quieter than that. I will warn Crookjaw that the hunters are coming and urge him to go as far as possible into the fast-nesses of the forest."

"I doubt if he will listen to you, Gildaen," he said, shaking his head. "When will the king be ready to ride?"

"Directly after they have broken their fast."

"What can I do?" Hickory asked earnestly.

"Show me how to find Crookjaw!"

"No more than that?"

"You risk death if you are discovered, Hickory. Evonna counsels you to stay hidden until the hunt is over."

"Hide like a coward when the king's life is in danger!" he said indignantly.

"Please be prudent," Gildaen pleaded. "Show me the path, Hickory. I must hurry!"

Gildaen knew that the big man was unhappy because he

could not be of greater service. His brow was furrowed, as if he were wrestling with a thorny problem.

"Look," he said when they reached the edge of the clearing. "See where the brush has been laid flat? And there he uprooted a young tree and shredded its trunk. He likes to destroy, that one! Head straight that way, dead west, until you come to a thicket of briers. The place is like a fortress in summer, a tangle of vines and creepers. It is one of the tusker's favorite hiding places. The bed of this stream flows close by, so you will have no trouble finding it. At your pace, a quarter of an hour should bring you there. Take care, Gildaen," he warned. "He is not a beast to be taken lightly!"

Gildaen was off and running even as Hickory finished speaking. He was happy simply to be out-of-doors again. The long confinement in the farmhouse, then in the wagon, and finally in the palace had made him forget how much he prized this freedom to stretch his legs and run. The sun was shining, the world was turning green, and it was easy to forget his mission. He felt fully alive, healthy, strong. The scent of a fox brought him back to a more sober mood. "I must move carefully," he thought. "There is no sense in watching out for the boar and being snatched up by a fox instead!" As he ran, he heard bits of conversation from the treetops, sometimes an argument between a returning family of birds and the squirrels who had taken over their quarters. The ground was covered with the soft needles of evergreens, and their pleasant scent surrounded him for a time until he emerged from their dark shadows into a more open woods. He had been watching for signs of Crookjaw, and these he had found along the way. Tender young plants had been uprooted. There were marks of his rooting in the leaf mold, and dirt thrown up

every which way. "Not very cautious," thought Gildaen.
"He must be quite sure of himself to be so bold." He
stopped and sniffed. A certain odor had been growing
stronger, not exactly a bad odor, but pungent and acrid.
"Not a pleasant fellow to be near," he thought. "Fancy
what Mignon would say to him!"

He knew that he must be close to the boar's lair. He
went slowly now, taking care not to break even a single
small twig as he advanced. Ahead of him was the brake of
brambles Hickory had mentioned. "There must be a back
entrance," he thought, and moved around cautiously. He
had almost circled back when he saw a place where a large
beast could make his way into the thicket by maneuvering
deftly. He could hear a wheezing now, regular and slow.
"He's in there all right!" he thought. He listened for a
few minutes more and realized that the boar must be
asleep. He stationed himself just a little closer to the boar's
sleeping place. He could see him now, lying on his side,
asleep on a soft bed of fallen leaves, rather like one of the
big palace hounds. Crookjaw did not look as fierce and terrible as Gildaen had expected him to.

He cleared his throat. "Master Crookjaw?" he said.

Instantly the boar was on his feet and looking around.
Gildaen was amazed at the way that unwieldy body roused
itself so quickly, and he began to understand why Hickory
had warned him not to take the boar lightly. Crookjaw
had caught a glimpse of him. His hide bristled with wiry
black hairs that gave him a warlike look. On either side
of his lower jaw wicked-looking tusks were set. He had his
head slightly down and to one side, gazing at Gildaen with
deep-set little eyes. They had a bloodshot gleam.

"Who dares awaken me?" he challenged in a gruff voice.
He stared hard at Gildaen, who stood poised for flight if

the boar should decide to charge. He knew that Crookjaw could never hope to catch him in the tangle of brambles and thorns. Evidently Crookjaw knew it too, for after he had pawed at the carpet of his bed, he stood stock-still, waiting. Gildaen thought that he might listen now.

"Master Crookjaw, my mistress sends you a warning."

The boar continued to stare, affording Gildaen the leisure to observe how he had come by his name. His lower jaw was badly twisted out of shape, so that his left tusk stuck out to the side. This peculiarity made him especially deadly, for any enemy attacking from that side had to stay well away from the crooked tusk, ready to hook or to gouge with a quick twist of the powerful head.

"How is it you can speak to me?" the boar grunted at last.

"My mistress gave me that power. It is she who sends you the warning."

"I need no warnings!" he said with a sniff and a grunt of disdain.

"The king's party seeks you today. They intend to hunt you down. You will be surrounded and trapped."

"Kings? Fah! What do I care for kings, you runt? They have hunted me before. By day and night for many years they have sought me. And they have often found me, too, but they paid for the finding!"

"Today they will not give up. You must leave here and go into the deepest thickets of the forest. Then they will seek in vain."

"Why were you sent here?"

"I was sent to help you escape in time."

Crookjaw smote the ground with his cloven hoof. "You lie. No one has ever wished to help me. I need no help."

Gildaen was worried. Crookjaw felt no fear about an

encounter with the king's men. In a way, the old boar appeared to be looking forward to such a meeting. He had escaped easily in the past, and he had slashed and gouged many a dog and hunter during these battles. Gildaen saw that his sides were scored with white, old scars that testified to his remarkable ability to survive the spears and the arrows of his enemies. Gildaen felt a grudging admiration for the old tusker. He had lived as he pleased, roamed where he wished, paying no heed to man or beast, obeying only his own moods. His cruel eyes showed that he cared for one being only—himself; himself and no other. He gloried in his strength and cunning. Gildaen wondered if he cared for any creature.

"Surely your family would not wish to see you trapped?" said Gildaen.

"Crookjaw has no more family. The weaklings died out long ago, and the strong are my enemies, as are all other beasts. They would like my lairs, my food, my hunting grounds. I will let none share my battles or my spoils." He gave a snort of contempt when he had said this.

"But it is not worth your time to fight with the king's men!"

"That is my business!"

Gildaen watched the tusker paw at his sleeping place. Talking to Crookjaw did no good. He would not listen to warnings, and certainly he would do no favors. It was useless to ask for his help. He had to get the boar out of this thicket and into the open, and then into the farthest reaches of the wood. "Perhaps," he thought, "I can trick him. He has a fierce temper."

He hopped a little closer and said, "My mistress should have known better!"

"What do you mean?" asked the boar suspiciously.

"She should have known that a stupid, loathsome animal such as you would not have sense enough to listen to reason."

"Stupid! Loathsome!" A spark of inner fire was kindled in the boar's little eyes.

"A rooter, a killer, a spoiler, who has to hide in the thorns!" taunted Gildaen.

"Come closer, rabbit!" snorted the boar, trying unsuccessfully to make his voice smooth. Gildaen could see that he was furiously angry.

"Worm-eater, grub-chewer," teased Gildaen, "hairy old hog!"

Several things happened at the same time. Crookjaw gave a grunt of blind rage and came charging through the thicket at him. Gildaen turned tail and raced out through the opening into the forest glade that bordered on the stream. A triumphant blast of horns sounded close at hand, together with the baying of excited hounds.

"They've come!" thought Gildaen, in a panic of uncertainty. "I am too late!" Even as he was thinking this thought, his feet were carrying him to the safety of the trees and bushes on the opposite side of the glade. Crookjaw stood in the center of the glade, blinking and searching for Gildaen. The fury in his brain had focused his thoughts on one object, catching and destroying the rabbit who had dared to call him such names. His usual wily caution was returning, but too late. Hounds came racing through the stream toward him, encircling him. The dogs were frantic with joy. They had brought to bay their old foe, and they were excited beyond measure at the thought of killing their quarry. One young spotted hound could not restrain himself. He plunged through the other dogs, seeking to end the hunt by himself. With a downward flick of his head, Crookjaw met the oncoming hound, caught him on that twisted tusk, and hurled him into the air. The spotted hound fell heavily to the earth, mortally wounded. He gave one low moan and was still. The others were maddened by the death of their fellow, but they had learned from his foolish example. They raced around and around Crookjaw, seeking the chance to dash in and seize him from behind. They were content, Gildaen saw, to keep the boar from escaping.

The young king, the Lord of the Bower, and several of his liegemen came riding across the stream. They rode straight for Crookjaw, their spears poised. As they passed among the dogs, Gildaen observed that Grimald deliberately rode his horse against the king's steed, Bayard, and gave him a sharp cut on the rump with his crop. Bayard, maddened by the sharp pain from the crop wielded by that feared hand, reared high into the air. At the same time, the Lord of the Bower spurred his own horse to rear and turn. He signaled to his fellows, and the others turned their horses at a gallop, as if the horses had panicked and were running away with their riders. King Justin had been ready to launch his spear when Bayard reared. Good horseman though he was, his heavy spear had unbalanced him in the saddle, and as the horse came down, he pitched forward and fell to the ground. His spear fell a few feet from where he landed.

When the hunters rode down upon him, Crookjaw was watching for a good opening through which to escape. Though he had bragged to Gildaen that he feared nothing and no one, yet he saw that the odds were against him if the hunters, too, could surround him. Suddenly all the men but one had galloped away again. That one had been thrown from his horse and lay dazed on the ground almost in front of him. Here was a helpless human. Now he would do the killing. He would gore him and shake him on his tusks and trample him under foot until there was nothing left of him. The maddened boar felt a surge of hot joy rush through him.

The young king looked up and saw the boar watching him, the lust for murder glimmering in those bloodshot eyes. His spear was not far away. He tried to get up, but his left leg was bent under him. He exerted himself with a mighty effort of will, but the pain was unbearable. He could not move. His companions were nowhere to be seen. The dogs had continued to circle the boar, and now they moved in close to their master, but Justin knew that they could not save him. Bayard, too, had returned to his master's side once the terror of Grimald's blow had subsided.

Crookjaw hesitated no longer. He charged the young man, but Bayard placed himself in front of his master, lashing out with his hooves at the advancing boar. Crookjaw moved to the side to escape the attack, slashing Bayard low on the flank as he went by. Blood gushed from the wound, and the horse whinnied in pain. The boar rushed by, almost into the circle of dogs, and then wheeled to charge again.

Gildaen felt utterly helpless. The hounds were wild with rage and frustration, watching for their chance but afraid to come too close to those deadly tusks and hooves. Gildaen felt sure that in the end Justin would be destroyed, and Bayard as well. Out of the corners of his eyes he saw someone dash past him and run into the glade. It was Hickory. He snatched up the king's spear and stood before him, his chest heaving with the effort of long, hard running.

"Are you hurt, sire?" he asked, pausing between words to gasp for breath.

"Hickory!" cried the young king. "Hickory, beware the boar!"

Crookjaw had seen the man race out of the woods and take up the spear. This human was going to try to cheat him of his rightful kill. His fury drove away any remaining caution. He would finish them both, spear or no spear. He lowered his head and charged. Hickory drew back his arm, and as the boar came at them, he plunged the spear into Crookjaw. The force of the boar's own charge helped to lodge the shaft. He screamed with pain and rage, changed direction slightly, and gored Hickory in the right thigh. The spear shaft snapped in Hickory's hand as he fell, wounded. The spearhead and four feet of the shaft were embedded in the flesh of Crookjaw's side; the rest remained in Hickory's hand.

Gildaen heard shouts and the sound of horses. The Lord Royce, leading the main body of hunters, swept across the stream. Crookjaw took one look at these reinforcements and decided he had had enough. His side throbbed painfully, and now he could no longer count on an easy kill. He charged the circle of dogs at its weakest point and dashed into the forest, pursued by the hounds.

In after days it was said that Crookjaw was in fact a demon who could not be killed by mortal hand, for hunters caught a glimpse of him now and again after he had sustained the wound that should have finished him off. The truth was that Crookjaw, that tenacious old tusker, recovered from his wound, though the spear remained in his side to the end of his long and quarrelsome days. Henceforth he avoided his old lairs and stayed far away from the palace and from the accustomed haunts of men.

Lord Royce and his men had formed a protective circle about the fallen king and Hickory. They dismounted quickly when the boar ran off.

"Staunch his wound," said the young king as Lord Royce bent over him. "My leg is broken, I think, but he is hurt far worse than I."

They tore a cloak and tied Hickory's wound tightly to stop the bleeding. Hickory was pale but managed to smile at the king.

"Just a scratch, sire," he said. "The boar escaped me, too!" he lamented.

"That is of no concern to me now, Hickory," said Justin.

At this moment the Lord of the Bower and his party of four came galloping up. Gildaen knew what they expected to find—the king lying dead and Lord Royce's men fighting the boar. The scene they found instead was plainly not going to be to their taste. The king was very much alive and speaking with the banished Hickory.

"Sire!" said Grimald, dismounting and entering the ring of hunters. "What does this mean? This arrant traitor, this poacher, here at your side!"

Gildaen had the satisfaction of observing that the king was looking at the Lord of the Bower with grave displeasure.

"If he had not been at my side, I would now be dead. He risked his life to save mine, and he has been gored."

The Lord of the Bower glanced down at Hickory's wound. For once, he had nothing to reply.

The king continued, accusingly, "Why were you not with me, my Lord of the Bower? Where were you and your liegemen when there was need of you?"

"Our horses bolted, your majesty," he answered smoothly. "We have only now conquered their craven hearts and beaten them to their senses."

"He lies, sire!" said Hickory, incensed beyond measure. "He lies as his black heart prompts him. He meant to see you killed!"

"Shall this knave have leave to speak against me, my lord king?" thundered the Lord of the Bower. "He is under pain of death for showing his miscreant face in your realm." He drew his sword. "I myself shall execute your sentence."

"Enough!" cried Justin. "Put up your sword. When I wish you to act for me, I shall say so!" Reluctantly the Lord of the Bower sheathed his sword. He gave Hickory a glance loaded with hatred.

Gildaen was alarmed. He did not know what course matters would take. The king was hesitant. He was hurt and confused, not sure what the wise course of action was. "If only," thought Gildaen, "Evonna was here!" But she was not. The king's men had gathered closer to him, facing the Lord of the Bower and his henchmen. The expression on their faces gave away their mutual hatred and distrust. King Justin gazed up at the circle of faces surrounding him. His eyes fell on Lord Royce.

"My lord," he said, addressing him with grave courtesy, "I must ask you for your counsel in this affair. It is true that I myself banished Hickory from my court and my realm, on pain of death. It is equally true that he has saved me from death today." There was almost a plea in his voice.

"Sire," answered Lord Royce, "since you would have my counsel, I will advise you. The charge against Hickory was never proven. It was his word against the word of others." Lord Royce raised his eyes and gazed into the cold eyes of his enemy. "He has proven his loyalty to you on many occasions, and today he has proven it again. Lift your sentence. Show him mercy."

"If you do that, my lord," said Grimald in his calm, deadly voice, "you prove yourself a weak king, a ruler who sways this way and that, unfit to rule a great kingdom such as this. Lawbreakers will say to themselves, 'The king will pardon us another day for the wrong we do today!' " Gildaen marveled at how Grimald had recovered his calmness and his icy poise. His words were powerful. They touched the king on his most vulnerable point, his desire to prove himself as a ruler. Gildaen was afraid that Justin would be convinced.

"I must think on this," said the king. His voice was weary. "Hickory is to be kept a prisoner for the time being, lest the people think their king cannot keep his word. But let his wound be looked to, and give him good food and care." He slumped back on the ground in a faint.

"What fools you are to argue while the king needs care!" said Hickory weakly. "You must attend to his leg."

"You are in no position to issue orders," snapped Grimald. "Seize him and throw him in the dungeons!" he ordered his men.

"Wait!" said Lord Royce. "The king said nothing of seizing. My men will convey him to the palace, and we shall also take the king with us."

Again the two men exchanged glances, dueling with their eyes. After this silent combat, the Lord of the Bower said with cool composure, "Have your way, old lord—for today!"

He and his men remounted and rode off. Gildaen stayed to see Hickory mounted behind one of the huntsmen. The unconscious king was lifted with the greatest care into the arms of one of Lord Royce's men. Then the party set off, the horses traveling at a walk, for the long ride back to the palace. Gildaen started off at top speed straight through the woods to bring Evonna the news.

IN THE DUNGEONS

HE EVENING MEAL WAS SERVED IN AN ATMO-
sphere of deep concern. Talk of the disas-
trous hunt engrossed the attention of the
court. The Lord of the Bower sat, as usual,
at the king's table, which was half empty
this evening. Only his liegemen sat with him. The knowledge had become common that he and his men had
deserted the king in his time of danger. Feelings long held
in check were coming out into the open as the courtiers
talked of what had taken place, and these feelings were
entirely unfriendly. Many had been afraid to speak against

the Lord of the Bower before, seeing how their king hung on his words, but now their anger and dislike were plainly written on their faces.

Gildaen had taken a place near the kitchen door to observe. Evonna had instructed him to watch the Lord of the Bower through the meal while she attended the king. Lord Royce had called for her as soon as the hunting party reached the palace, but before she went to the king, she sent Fara to the kitchens to help her uncle and dispatched Gildaen to the great hall.

When at last the dried fruits and nuts were being served, Gildaen wondered if he might return to the Walloons' quarters to await Evonna. He had not fully recovered from the shocks of the day. Just as he had traversed the last hedge that separated the forest from the palace grounds, a flash of orange jumped after him. The instant he came through the hedge, he felt himself changed back into his cat shape, as Evonna had told him he would be. He was grateful that the change had taken place without any mistake this time, for the next instant Dauber came crashing out of the brush, only to stop in amazement at the sight of him.

"It's you!" he growled in disgust. "My eyes are playing tricks on me. You are always coming out of nowhere."

Gildaen made no comment. He was enjoying Dauber's discomfiture.

"I could have sworn you were a rabbit," he grumbled, slouching off in the direction of the stables. Gildaen had raced on again to seek Evonna.

The nobles were leaving their tables, huddled in small groups, well away from where the Lord of the Bower sat. Gildaen could catch the name "Hickory" being repeated.

Throughout the meal the Lord of the Bower had engaged in conversation with Growze and the others. If he was alarmed, he certainly gave no sign of it. "Hard as ice, and as cold," thought Gildaen.

He simply could not wait any longer. The next time a servingman went back with his load, Gildaen slipped into the kitchen with him. Rustrim greeted him with a nod and went back to feasting on the leavings that had been put down for him. Gildaen saw that the Walloons were already directing the cleaning up. Fara was not in the kitchen. He hurried through the corridor that led back to their quarters and meowed softly at the door of the Walloons' rooms.

The door was opened by Fara. Evonna was with her.

"Well?" asked Gildaen. "Do not keep me in suspense!"

Evonna's face had been grave, but she smiled at his impatience.

"I am glad to find you the same, Gildaen!" she said. "Palace life has changed no whit of your impatience, although today I can excuse your haste. The young king is more fortunate than he knows. Instead of being a carcass tonight, he is safe in his chambers, but his left leg is broken. I have made him as comfortable as may be, and I have given him a sleeping draft. Still, many weeks will pass before he rides again or walks without aid."

"How is it that you were summoned, Evonna?" Fara asked.

"When Lord Royce and I met the other day, I told him of my skill in healing. The other nobles believe me to be a herb-wife, a village woman with long years of practice in caring for the sick. As luck would have it, the king's own physician was called back to Castelmaine. He will not return for at least a week, and I shall have the king on the road to recovery by then."

"What of Hickory?" asked Gildaen.

"I visited him next, pretending of course that I had never seen him before. I cleaned his wound. It is not as deep as I feared, and he is otherwise well."

"Where is he? Is he here in the palace?" asked Fara.

"More accurate to say under the palace. The king's orders were to place him in the dungeons, and there he is. His cell is not the lowest nor the blackest; a cell it remains, however. Damp, cold, and with little light."

Fara stamped her foot. "How can the king treat him so shamefully after he saved his life!"

"Hickory was banished on pain of death. The king would have been acting justly had he ordered Hickory killed on the spot. He wishes to act mercifully and would probably have done so, Gildaen tells me, had not the Lord of the Bower made him believe his subjects would despise him for a weakling. In the eyes of the law, Hickory is a criminal," Evonna reminded her.

"We know that he committed no crime—that everything was a plot of—that man's!" Fara retorted angrily.

"Evonna," said Gildaen, remembering the talk in the dining hall. "The nobles were talking about Hickory at dinner tonight, and it is plain they are on his side. I believe they all hate Grimald."

"I am sure of that, Gildaen. They have been afraid of him—until today."

"But, Evonna," protested Fara. "Matters stand worse now than before. The king has a broken leg and can't get away from the Lord of the Bower, and poor Hickory is wounded and locked away!"

Evonna lit the candle on the table. The dusk had come as they talked. A bird was singing in the twilight, singing of the nest he had made in the branches of a cherry tree and of the new eggs in the nest. Gildaen could not feel utterly downcast. The spring had come and, with it, a quickening of hope.

"You know," Evonna replied thoughtfully, "I do not share your view, Fara. We are better off, I think, than before. The Lord of the Bower knows he is under suspicion. If anything should happen to Justin, the blame would fall on him. For the same reason, he cannot do Hickory harm. The courtiers are openly against him; he and his men will be closely watched. Before, everything was in their favor. Now I believe we have a chance, thanks to Hickory's courage. For once, I am glad that my advice was cast aside."

"I wish I could see Hickory!" said Fara.

"That can be arranged," replied Evonna, taking up her apron from the back of a chair. "I have been granted permission to bring food to him. The king said, remember, that he was to be well treated. You may come with me, Fara, and carry the tray."

"Thank you!" Fara said. "Can we go right away, please?"

"What about me?" asked Gildaen.

"I see no reason why our cat should not trail along behind us when we make our visit," said Evonna.

"Nor do I!" exclaimed Gildaen, well pleased.

They heard footsteps in the corridor, and the door was opened by Walter Walloon.

"Well, mistress?" he asked, his face drawn with worry. "What of our young king? How does he? Will he live?"

"Walter!" reproved his wife, coming in behind him. "Give Mistress Evonna time to draw a breath!"

"The king sleeps," Evonna replied. "His leg is broken, but it will mend."

"I was sure he was done for!" he cried. "What of Hickory then? Has he succumbed to his wound?"

Gildaen thought with some annoyance that Fara's uncle had a way of seeing and saying the blackest.

"I was just on my way to prepare him a tray," Evonna answered.

"A tray? Is he not in the dungeons? Is he not wounded unto death?" Walter Walloon asked in a rush.

Evonna assured him that Hickory was doing well and that the king himself had given orders for Hickory to have good care.

"Don't you remember, Walter?" asked his wife. "Hickory saved the king's life!"

"Yes, yes, now that you mention it, Wilma, I do. I have been so distraught since we heard the news that I hardly know what to say or think. Take what you will from the larders, Mistress Evonna." When he saw Fara's eager look, he added, "You go along too, my dear."

"Yes, Uncle!" she said, giving him a kiss as she went by. Nothing could have pleased her more than for him to issue such an invitation.

Gildaen slipped out with his friends. The kitchens had been set in order for the night. The long wooden tables were clean. The fires had been banked, the spits cleaned, and two boys were still at work sweeping the stone floor. Rustrim was curled up in his usual place near the hearth, looking fatter and more contented even than usual. "He will kill himself with eating at this rate," Gildaen thought. Rustrim did not even bother to open his eyes as they moved past him. In the pastry larder Evonna found a meatpie not yet cold. She moved on and took half a loaf of wheaten bread, cut a chunk of cheese, and drew a mug of ale from the keg that had been broached for the evening meal. She arranged these on a tray, and they made their way back to the main corridor through the scullery. Evonna stopped at the quarters of the palace housekeeper, and with a little persuasion that woman entrusted two blankets to Fara's arms. A long passageway led them to the south wing of the palace. They crossed a narrow courtyard to another, separate building and came to a tunnel that turned downward.

They were going underground, winding around and around. "Like being inside a snail shell," thought Gildaen. There was a guard stationed at each full turn. The guards nodded them on, having seen Evonna pass earlier and not deeming Fara or Gildaen worth noticing. Gildaen tried to look as idle and unconcerned as a cat should. He doubted if any prisoner could make his escape from this place.

There were no graceful tapers burning in these corridors. Instead, rush lights flickered and hissed, making the air hazy with smoke. Gildaen felt as if they were walking an unending circle into the bowels of the earth. He could imagine how a prisoner must feel as he descended lower and lower, leaving behind the light and the clean air. He had counted nine downward circles when the ground became level and they saw ahead of them a massive gate that stretched from floor to ceiling. Behind this gate were the cells.

A jailer sat in front of the gate, his supper before him on a table. As they approached, he sighed heavily, a man who sees more work coming.

"I suppose you will be wanting the gate opened *again?*" he asked Evonna accusingly. "Never a minute to myself!" he muttered. "Always at beck and call." He hoisted himself unwillingly out of his chair and fumbled for the great key that hung on the ring at his waist. The jailer appeared to have tumbled into ashes and never to have gotten properly cleaned off again. His hair was unkempt, his moustaches drooped, and his uniform was so creased and rumpled that Gildaen was sure he must sleep in it. He wondered if the man thought that being down here in the dark no one would see him.

The jailer opened the gate for them and propped it with a stone wedge. "Work, work, always work," he grumbled as he led them in. Five of these first cells were occupied. The prisoners, wearing clothes that might once have been palace finery, watched them with a hopeless look that made Gildaen despair for Hickory. Evonna dropped back a few paces and said in a guarded voice, "These men are all courtiers who have displeased Grimald in some way."

The jailer led them past many empty cells until they came to the very last, where on the floor Hickory lay on a pile of straw. The jailor went through his keys twice before he found the right one. "Call when you are ready," he said, locking them in with Hickory. Evonna put her finger to her lips and shook her head. None of them spoke until the jailor had shuffled away and was safely back in front of the gate again.

Hickory sat up on one elbow, regarding them with obvious pleasure.

Fara bent down next to him, setting down her blankets. "Oh, Hickory!" she said, gazing at his drawn face. "I hate to see you lying on the damp straw!"

"Don't forget, Fara," Hickory replied, "that I slept on straw in the barn at your farm. If it were only the straw, I would not care." He hung his head.

The tears rolled silently down Fara's cheeks as she knelt there. Evonna touched her shoulder firmly. "No time for that," she said sternly. "Nor for despondency," she chided, turning her gaze on Hickory. "Eat your dinner, my friend, and let us talk, for our time here must be short."

She helped Hickory to sit up and prop himself against one blanket, and then she covered him with the other.

"Gildaen, is it you?" Hickory asked, addressing the handsome gray cat.

"Gildaen, at your service!" he replied, sitting down directly in front of his friend.

"You have become courtly," Hickory said, chuckling.

"Thank you!" said Gildaen. "But compliments aside, Hickory, I have found out that there are many in the palace who would like to help you."

Evonna nodded. "Lord Royce told me that there are those who are ready to oust the Lord of the Bower at the first chance. They are still afraid, but they are willing to make some attempt."

"This news is better even than the food you have brought. Tell me, Evonna, how is my young master? How is King Justin?"

"He is asleep, and he is safe. Lord Royce himself will watch at his bedside, and when he is weary, one of his men will take his place. I think Grimald will wait before he makes the next attempt."

"Do you really think he will try again?" asked Fara. "Isn't there a chance that he will leave?"

"I think not. He has tasted power, and he desires to have the rule of this kingdom. But he is prudent. He will wait and plan and make sure that his next attempt does not go awry."

"Then Hickory is not safe either!" Fara said. "What can we do?"

Evonna motioned to her to keep her voice low. "Hickory," she asked, "have you heard of the Witch of Mallyn?"

"A witch?" asked Gildaen fearfully. "Is she in league with the Lord of the Bower?"

"No, Gildaen," Hickory replied, "she is not evil."

"Lord Royce said that she might be persuaded to help us," Evonna explained. "Justin's mother was her friend, and she herself is godmother to the young king. She used to visit the court on occasion, and I have heard she did only good works when she came. Her name was held in high esteem, but she has not been here since the old king died. Lord Royce said this lady has great power for good and is learned in the healing arts. He believes that once she knows the king's life is at stake, she will leave her seclusion and come here. If anyone can outwit Grimald, Lord Royce believes she can."

"How is she to learn of his plight?" asked Fara.

"Gildaen and I will make the journey to her home," said Evonna. "We will wait a few more days until I see that Hickory's wound is mending as it should."

"I will come, too," said Fara.

"Not this time," said Evonna kindly. "We could not explain to your aunt and uncle why you wanted to leave. And you must take on the task of bringing food to Hickory and giving him news of the king."

Gildaen was thinking that he did not relish another trip so soon, especially to meet a witch, no matter how kindhearted she was reputed to be.

Fara shook her head. "I hope she knows how to deal with Grimald," she said. "How far away is this witch?"

"She dwells in a cottage to the north of the king's forest. There is no road, but Lord Royce has given me directions."

"Psssst! Gildaen!" hissed a voice behind them. Gildaen spun around and saw Scudder, his black head pressed against the bars, his eyes alight with urgency.

"What is it?" asked Gildaen. "How did you know I was here?"

"Don't be silly!" replied the black-and-white cat.

"There's a cat who sits just out of sight at the entrance to the dungeons. I had only to do a little inquiring to find you. I have a message for you from Mignon. She overheard the Lord of the Bower tell his henchmen that in three days he would be master of the palace!"

"How?" demanded Gildaen.

"He has sent for a friend who will pretend to be a famous physician. He will ask to see the king and prescribe for him—a lethal poison! Then he will pretend that he was too late to help and that the bungling of your friend Evonna brought about the king's death. Evonna will be executed, and the Lord of the Bower will seize the throne!"

Gildaen was stunned. Evonna said quietly, "It would appear that I was wrong. Grimald is very greedy." She told Hickory and Fara what the cat Scudder had relayed.

"We must leave at dawn, Gildaen," said Evonna. "I will inform Lord Royce of this plan, but I doubt if he will be able to keep the king from seeing the impostor."

"Give my thanks to Mignon," said Gildaen to Scudder, remembering his manners, "and ask her to keep watch."

"The palace cats will do their part!" answered Scudder, and dashed away.

THE WITCH OF MALLYN

HE NEXT MORNING, BEFORE DAYBREAK, THEY were ready to leave. Evonna was mounted on a young mare Hace the groom had picked out for her. Gildaen, once more in his own shape, was hidden in his wicker basket, which was securely fastened to the saddle.

Hace had asked Evonna, "What do you think, ma'am? Any chance of gettin' Hickory out of the lockup?"

Evonna answered quietly, "We will make sure he has a chance." She asked him to speak to Fara whenever he could and to give her help if she should need it, which he readily agreed to do.

Then they were off. Polly, the mare, responded to Evonna's voice and light touch with such an obliging spirit that they were soon out of sight of the palace and riding along the oak-lined road. The morning was mist-laden, white and mysterious. They could hear the birds calling to one another, but they could not see them; even the oaks appeared as ghostly shadows looming on either side. Gildaen had lifted his head after they passed the guards at the gates, and now he gazed out into the shimmering morning mist, thinking about the day ahead. He knew that Evonna counted heavily on this meeting with the Witch of Mallyn. She seemed loath to deal directly with the Lord of the Bower lest he prove the more powerful of the two. He was curious, as well, about the witch's dwelling, for no one had been able to tell them anything of it other than its location; no one at the palace had ever dreamed of approaching it closely. Evonna kept the mare to a gentle canter, so regular and flowing that Gildaen was rocked to and fro as if he were in a cradle.

The fog began to dissolve. First they could see a haze of sunlight. A few moments more and the trees stood outlined in warm morning gleam, their leaves a freshly washed green. The forest looked new, bursting with the vigor of spring growth. Gildaen felt he could almost see the leaves unfurl and the grasses turn a warmer green along the road.

They had ridden east, pretending their destination was the village of King's Riding but intending to strike north as soon as they came to the edge of the forest. In that way they could ride through meadowland almost all the way. The columns of oaks came to an end, and the road

changed once more from a carefully groomed royal roadway to a bumpy dirt wagon track.

"One can see," Evonna remarked, "that the king does
not ride in this direction often, though the village we
supposedly will visit is known as King's Riding!"

"I'm glad we needn't go on!" said Gildaen, imagining
the jolts and bruises such a road would inflict.

Evonna brought Polly to a halt. She turned the mare
back in the direction from which they had just come. She
sat silently for several minutes, listening.

"Why are we waiting?" asked Gildaen.

"I want to make sure we are not being followed," she
answered.

"You think *he* might have had us watched?" Gildaen
asked, alarmed.

"Who knows?" she answered. "I am certain he keeps
track of comings and goings. I think it is safe to move on
now."

With a gentle movement on the rein, she turned the
mare north, along the skirts of the forest. The sun was on
their right, and every trace of fog and mist had disappeared. Gildaen could hardly bear to look to the east, so
brilliant was the light shining on field and mead. They
found stretches where they could make good time, land
bare and flat, not yet overgrown with weed and vine, as
it would be in a few months. Other times they had to pick
their way through thorn and scrub that reached out to
poke and scratch at the horse's flanks.

The forest on their left was filled with noise and activity, as the animals and birds busied themselves with
building anew and repairing what the winter had destroyed. The woods, thought Gildaen, were even more
abustle than the palace kitchen before a meal.

By midday the mare was sweating and Evonna had taken off her shawl. A stream that issued from the woods sparkled invitingly. Much to Gildaen's pleasure, Evonna halted the mare. "Time to stop for a bit," she said. Lifting Gildaen from the basket, she commented, "You have never been so heavy before. Life in the palace has made you fat, Gildaen."

Gildaen was insulted at first, but he had to admit that the daily bowls of rich milk had done something to his weight.

"I suppose," he said with a sigh, "that I was lucky to leave! But the life of a cat is not as horrid as I once thought. Not horrid at all, now that I recall it. Still, it is better to be me than a glutton of a cat like Rustrim!"

They drank from the cold water of the brook and refreshed themselves, while Polly grazed contentedly. Gildaen found a carpet of violets growing at the feet of the oaks on the bank. The leaves were tender and the flowers quite delicious. Nothing he had eaten in a long time satisfied him as much as did this spring repast.

When Evonna put him back in his basket, he was aware that he was ready to fall asleep: the sun on his fur, the feeling of fullness in his stomach, and the easy, rocking gait of the mare lulled him. His troubles seemed at the moment far away. He drifted into slumber, a lazy afternoon nap that lasted until he had a confused dream of being faced by a monster with eyes like lanterns and dozens of hands. He let out an "Oh!" and woke up.

"You squealed as if you had been stuck with a pin, Gildaen!" remarked Evonna.

Gildaen blinked, trying to remember where he was. He saw that they were still riding north and that Evonna was sitting, relaxed, her hands lightly holding the reins. Since he had met the owl in the ruined castle garden, his life had been one adventure after another, until it was hard to tell where dreams began and reality left off.

"Tell me what is troubling you?" she asked.

"I don't understand it myself," he replied. "I am muddled. In my dream you were a monster. At least, I think it was you, and I suppose it was a dream."

"A monster?" She laughed. "Not very complimentary! But never mind that." She turned to look around at him as if to reassure herself. "You have gone through a great deal in a short space of time, my friend. Others bigger and sturdier than you might have faltered where you have not. Your heart, your mind, your courage have been tested more than once. I think you have become more than you were before, but it is little wonder that you sometimes feel confused."

These words were comforting to Gildaen. He felt that he had been changing—not only from one form to another, but inside himself—and the changing was not easy. He glanced to the left and saw that the forest was etched in gold as the afternoon light filtered through the tangle of trees.

"Most humans hunt for the barren, cold metal they call gold. They guard it jealously and steal it from their fellows. They never notice the real gold which sets the grass and trees to quickening and reaching for the sky," Evonna commented, as if she were reading his thoughts.

She guided the horse slightly to the west. They had come to the northern reaches of the forest. The trees stopped suddenly, as if at a border beyond which they could not go. There were miles of meadow and grassland ahead of them. At the edge of the woods, a carpet of hare-bells was spread; the blue wild flowers were like soft jewels in a setting of green. The plain rose and fell, a series of grassy waves across which they rode: first down into a trough from whose bottom Gildaen could no longer look back and see the forest, then up again. When they reached the top of the next hill, they saw, far away still, what looked like a small grove. Within that grove was the cottage of the witch! They traveled on in silence, admiring the beauty of the scene but thinking ahead to the meeting soon to come.

The approach to the grove took them almost an hour. The view was deceptive, for there were many rolling hills of meadowland to cross before they were really near it. Gildaen could understand why the Witch of Mallyn had chosen this spot for her home. From the privacy of the trees she could look out and see every approach. No one could come upon her by surprise. He was sure that she had been watching their progress ever since they rode to the top of the first hill. He wondered what she looked like and thought that they should have asked Lord Royce to describe her in order to distinguish her from her servants or companions.

When they were within easy walking distance of the trees, Evonna drew rein. The mass of greenery they had seen first could now be made out as high hedges. Within the green walls were tall trees and the roof and chimney of the witch's cottage. There was a twittering in the air.

"She doesn't seem to care about making a great show," Gildaen said to Evonna.

The high hedges were in first flower, bearing blossoms of white and lavender. The fragrance of these lilacs was borne to them on the evening breeze. An archway of white wicker covered with climbing vines provided the only entrance. Gildaen sniffed the lilacs with delight. As he gazed at the grove, he believed for the first time what Lord Royce had told Evonna—the Witch of Mallyn was not evil. Surely no wicked sorceress could live in this place.

Evonna dismounted. "Stay here, Gildaen," she commanded. She walked toward the archway, while Gildaen watched, a trifle anxiously. When she reached the path that led under the archway, she stopped. The twittering had grown louder suddenly. From the hedges and from the trees in the grove, birds arose, hundreds of them. There were linnets, starlings, song sparrows, larks, thrushes, nightingales, and birds Gildaen did not recognize, of every hue of the rainbow. Gildaen was frightened, for they were making straight for Evonna. They settled on her, some in her hair, some on her arms, and those who had no perch flew about her head. Gildaen thought she would be pecked to death in less than a moment.

But the birds were not attacking her. They sat as light and as docile as butterflies on a flower, all chattering and twittering at once, so Gildaen could not make out a word of what they were saying. Evonna raised her head and laughed, gay peals of the happiest laughter Gildaen had ever heard.

"My dear friends and watchmen!" she exclaimed to the birds who surrounded her. "I thank you for your welcome!" Turning to the horse, Evonna whistled coaxingly. Polly trotted forward; the many birds made her nervous.

"My friends have reminded me of who I am—at last! We need have no further fear, Gildaen. You are looking at the Witch of Mallyn."

"Where?" asked Gildaen apprehensively. He did not understand.

"Right in front of you. Don't you hear, Gildaen? *I* am the Witch of Mallyn!"

Gildaen was thunderstruck. He could hardly believe
what Evonna had told him, but the next instant he knew
it was true. They had come here, led by their pressing
need, to the one spot where Evonna could find herself
again. He felt a great desire to jump from the mare's
back and run wildly through the clover. As it was, he did
nothing but sit where he was and feel joyful, for words
failed him utterly.

The birds circled over their heads, commenting on
Gildaen and the mare. Polly put her ears back and
neighed unhappily. Gildaen saw now that the birds were
friendly and that they were the watchmen of Evonna's
gate. They were escorted to the white arch by the birds,
who left them when they passed under it. Evonna had
taken the bridle and was leading the mare, who was much
more at ease now that the birds had gone back to their
homes in the hedges and trees.

Inside was a sight that gave Gildaen a sense of peace
and order, a homecoming to a place never seen before,
which seemed familiar and comforting nonetheless. In the
center of a grove of ancient trees stood the whitewashed
stone cottage whose roof and chimney they had seen from
outside the hedges. On either side of the path that led to
it, and surrounding the cottage, were garden plots. There
were gardens filled with spring flowers in full bloom,
masses of yellow, coral, lavender, and red. The colors were
of such a purity and intensity of hue that they lit up the
twilight. There were kitchen gardens, Gildaen was happily
noticing; he could make out rows of neat lettuces and the
cheerful tops of radishes and scallions. He was acutely
hungry once again. His nose was tickled by the smell of
aromatic herbs, planted by patterns in raised beds. He
could see no traces of neglect anywhere and wondered

who had cared for these gardens so well in Evonna's absence. Trellises of purple-flowered vines were thriving on both sides of the cottage, while ivy twined lovingly over the wall in front.

A flock of white doves flew from their nesting places in the ivy, cooing "Welcome! Welcome!" in soft voices. Gildaen felt this was the first truly peaceful place he had ever known, a haven. There was a tranquillity here that drained away sorrow and alarm. The circling hedges shut out every woe, leaving the spirit to rejoice in a garden world where time had no meaning. Gildaen could not have put any of these feelings into words. Words were not necessary here.

Evonna opened the cottage door, and the room came to life, as if it had been asleep and waiting for her return. A fire kindled itself in the hearth. A flowered cloth shook itself smooth on the table. Delicate plates and a setting for two flew out of the cupboard and arranged themselves on the cloth.

"Did you do that?" asked Gildaen, awed by this strange room.

"In a way I did, Gildaen. I can do things here in my home that I would not care to do elsewhere." She laughed, and Gildaen saw the years slip from her face. She was Evonna no longer, but herself. The face was neither young nor old, but harmonious and beautiful, ageless. Her hair, the color of ripe wheat, fell in soft tendrils about her face. She was clad now in a simple gown of soft white wool with flowing sleeves. What Gildaen saw in her face was what he had felt when he first looked through the archway. He saw made visible before him the strength, the calmness, the wisdom he had admired in her from the time they first met.

"Be at home, Gildaen," she said, taking the basket he had traveled in for so long and going out once more. Gildaen surveyed the room. The floor was of smooth stone, covered by rugs of thick wool in bright colors. There were tall windows on three sides that gave onto the gardens. He remembered that he had thought the Witch of Mallyn spent her time spying on those who approached, and he realized that from none of these windows could one see anything of the outside world. A table stood by the fire, and on the opposite side of the hearth was a cleverly carved rocking chair whose back and arms were worked in the shapes of vines and flowers. Under the windows were tables, two of which were filled with crocks and jars of every size, labeled in a bold hand. There were also several mortar and pestle combinations in varying sizes, measuring cups, and wooden canisters. The third table was piled high with books, leather-bound, of every description. A number of these were well worn, reflecting long years of constant use.

When the Lady of Mallyn returned, her basket was filled with freshly picked vegetables and flowers.

"Tonight you shall taste of my hospitality, Gildaen. This is the first time since we have been together that I can offer you something of my own!"

A bouquet of bright yellow oxlips glowed like a second fire on the table. She put down a napkin on the floor near her place at table and arranged what she had picked for him on one of her delicate plates. She fetched honey cakes from a cupboard and broke one into pieces for Gildaen. He thought that the taste was like the gathered sweetness of a summer's day in the meadow.

"It grows dark," she said, and fat candles sprang into flame on the tables and shelves. "I can afford as many of these fine candles as I need," she said. "My bees make more than enough wax to give me light and a sufficiency of the honey you have just savored."

"Evonna," said Gildaen hesitatingly, "what shall I call you from now on?" He had been puzzling over this question since he felt full enough to think of something other than food.

She placed dried leaves in a pot and poured boiling water over them. A flowery and spicy aroma rose up as the brew steeped.

"Call me what you will, Gildaen. Most people call me the Lady of Mallyn, or the Witch of Mallyn, as they please. I have taken many names and shapes, as you know! Use any that please you."

"I'll continue to call you Evonna then," replied Gildaen. "I've gotten used to it."

She sipped a cup of the herb tea whose fresh scent perfumed the room. Gildaen thought that he would be perfectly content if his other friends were well and safe. The room was bathed in a soft yet vivid light that made each object appear fine and precious. The Lady of Mallyn was surrounded by this warm radiance, which came as much from within her, Gildaen thought, as from the light around her.

"Gildaen," she said softly, breaking the peaceful silence, "there are but two days left before Grimald's plot is ripe. We must consider what is to be done."

"Before we make a plan, Evonna, will you tell me how you came to be an owl? Do you remember?"

"Yes, quite clearly. You will find that the Lord of the Bower is a part of the story, and it is a long one. Are you comfortable?"

He nodded, happily at ease on a soft woolen rug. She sat down close by in her rocking chair.

"You remember that the Witch of Mallyn was god-

mother to the young prince Justin? His dear mother was
my friend. Before she married and took up her duties as a
queen, she studied herblore and gardencraft with me. She
was very happy when her little son was born, and indeed I
thought him a fine child. When the prince was ten years
old, I went away on one of my wanderings in search of
new plants. When I returned, I learned the queen had
died suddenly.

"I then made it my business to visit the palace as
often as I could, spending time with the prince. I was
forced to travel again, two years ago, in answer to a sum-
mons from an old friend who required my assistance. Last
summer I came home and found that the king had been
stricken by the same affliction that took the life of his
queen. I learned, too, that Justin was attended by
Grimald, who had come to court for a long stay. I disguised myself in order to find out what he was up to. I
have known of his evil ways many a long year. Soon I saw
that Justin was no longer making use of his father's faithful counselors and that the enchanter had flattered and
beguiled him into obedience. I knew I had to act. I began
to suspect Grimald had somehow contrived the death of
the king and queen, carefully, taking his time so no one
would realize the truth."

"But how?" interrupted Gildaen, horrified.

"The Lord of the Bower has an interest in gardens as
well as I, Gildaen. He takes his name from the enchanted
garden within his fortress, filled with flowers and plants
such as you have probably never beheld."

"I can't imagine him growing flowers!" he burst out.

"These flowers," said the Lady of Mallyn, "are very like
him. Each is poisonous. He uses his skill and knowledge—
and never deceive yourself that he does not possess both—
to breed new plants, strange hybrids of matchless beauty

and strength, but not a one is wholesome. From their pollen, their seeds, or their leaves or roots he makes his drugs, philters, and powders. I have heard that there is always a stream of travelers coming and going from that fortress, bringing him gold in exchange for what they buy. He is known throughout many lands for these brews and poisons of his. He has immense wealth, Gildaen, because of the cutthroats and ruffians who find their way to his gates. As long as he was content to make his mischief from his stronghold, I took little notice of him. But he seems to have wearied of limited sway. He may have decided that ruling a kingdom is more to his taste!"

"You believe he poisoned the king and queen?" Gildaen asked.

"That is exactly what I thought and still do think. I took the form of a plain small bird, a song sparrow, and flew to his fortress. The journey is not difficult, only half a day's flight to the west and north.

"I flew over the high walls into his enchanted garden. I thought I was high enough up so that the perfumes of the plants would not affect me. I began to feel drowsy, and indeed I could hardly move my wings. Even though I should have known better, I flew down to perch in a fruit tree. Those foul plants of his, I knew, had different effects: some poison quickly, some are slow-acting, and others have the power to cloud the memory. What I did not know was that the fragrance of the flowers had these same properties. I must have closed my eyes and dozed off.

"When I awoke, I had no idea who I was or where I was. I had forgotten that part of my art which comes from long study and requires memory for completion, but nothing could take away my special art, which is to change myself as the need arises.

"It is a great stroke of luck that I was not discovered and

that he seems not to have learned of my misfortune. How he would have triumphed! And made sure that I never regained my memory! Perhaps I would even now be sitting in a cage in his fortress," she said reflectively.

Gildaen was horrified at the thought.

"He has made no attempt to destroy my grove, which he might have done if he had known of my plight."

"I think the birds would have kept it safe," said Gildaen, remembering the huge flock of birds in the hedges.

"Yes, I think so, too," she said, smiling. "They are gentle songsters, but they allow none to pass save those they recognize as friends."

"The Lord of the Bower is behind all our troubles!" said Gildaen. "The only good that has come out of it, for me at least, is that I met you."

"You may not think so in a little while!" warned Evonna.

"No matter what comes, lady, I am glad to be with you. I think you have already made up your mind about what we should do."

"There is no choice. We must have his talisman."

"You speak in riddles. What is a talisman?"

"Gildaen, every enchanter has a talisman or token, an ancient object from time-out-of-mind about which he has wound his spells for ages."

"Can we catch him sleeping and find it?" Gildaen asked.

"He would never be so foolish as to keep it on his own person. And searching a sorcerer would not prove an easy task, Gildaen. No," she said, rocking slowly in her chair, "I am sure he keeps it in the garden rather than in the fortress. It was this talisman I was seeking when I fell victim to the poisonous blooms in the garden. Have I explained, Gildaen, that the bower is within the garden?"

"Aren't they the same thing?" he asked. "Is the bower different from the garden?"

"The bower is in the center of the garden, the inner-most portion, the heart of his magic."

"Even *you* failed to enter it," said Gildaen mourn-fully.

"But *you* must not," she answered, gazing at him. What Gildaen saw in her eyes made the tips of his ears tingle and chilled him, though he sat close to the fire.

"You mean—you mean," he faltered, "that I am to seek this talisman?"

"You must find it and destroy it if you can. Or you must try to bring it to me," she answered. "Once we have it, I am convinced that his power over the king will be gone and that the wicked creatures he keeps in thrall will desert him or turn against him."

"Will he die?" whispered Gildaen.

"I doubt it. But his future days will prove no menace to others."

"I am afraid," confessed Gildaen in a small voice.

"If there were another way, I would choose it. Our time grows short, and our friends need help."

"But, Evonna, how am I to find this talisman? How am I to know what it is?"

She poured herself another cup of the tea. "I am not sure," she murmured, almost to herself. "I am not sure, although I have given long thought to the matter." Her eyes seemed to be looking far past him and the room. "Yes," she said. "It will certainly be disguised as quite an ordinary thing. Some little difference will give it away." Her eyes came back to him. "You must be observant. Bear in mind that he must keep his servants from stealing it. They are as likely to steal from him as they are from another if they think they can escape punishment. There-fore, the talisman must be cleverly hidden. Because he is cunning, he will have it displayed in plain sight, knowing that most thieves look for a concealed treasure, not one on view to all." She said reassuringly, "You will sense what it is, Gildaen, I am sure of it. You have an instinct for the right choice, as I've known from the first."

Gildaen thought numbly that he would need more than instinct to protect him from the wiles of the enchanter and from the flowers and trees of the garden. His ears dropped low as these unpleasant thoughts occurred to him. He would try not to prove a coward, not after the adventures he had come through and not when the lives of his friends depended on his courage.

The Lady of Mallyn seemed, as always, to have guessed his thoughts. "Do not think, Gildaen, that I will send you defenseless into the enchanter's garden. I promise that you will be equal to the task. In fact, I think that you will hardly recognize yourself," and she gave a laugh that was almost mischievous at a joke she was not yet ready to share with him.

"You had better try to sleep now," she urged. She lined his basket with a soft shawl, and into this he gladly jumped. He was tired, and his thoughts began to wander. He remembered that on the morrow he was to go to the bower, and then he thought of mornings he had played with his sisters and brothers in the clover on his hill. He could see the Lady of Mallyn seated again in her rocking chair. In her lap was a thick book through which she slowly paged. Other books from the shelves were piled be-side her chair on the floor. Gildaen closed his eyes.

HAWKS

E WAS RUNNING, RUNNING, RUNNING TO ESCAPE the birds that pursued him, doubling on his tracks, searching frantically for a wall with an opening, or a thicket, but there was nothing. Even the grass was too short to afford him cover. They were directly over him, cawing and shrieking, diving toward him, when at last, by a tremendous effort of will, he forced himself awake. His heart was pounding in his throat as he opened his eyes and saw the comforting whitewashed walls of the Lady of Mallyn's cottage.

The sun was streaming through the tall windows. He

wondered guiltily how late it was and marveled at how long he had slept. There was some task that needed doing today, and now it might be too late to get a good start. Then he remembered the talk of the night before, and the familiar thrill of fear shot through him. This was the day!

He hopped up onto one of the wide window ledges. The window was open, and the sounds and smells of the gardens outside were wafted in on the tide of a morning breeze. Everything was even more beautiful in the rich light of this spring morning than it had been at twilight. Finches were celebrating the glory of the day, performing rolls and spirals in the air. They were chattering about the return of their mistress. Gildaen felt that every living being in the circle of her flowering hedges was rejoicing. He alone felt the heavy weight of the future hanging over him. "Just when there's a reason to feel glad," he thought, "there's something to spoil it."

The door was swung wide by the Lady of Mallyn, dressed in a gown of pale green.

"I have your breakfast here, Gildaen," she called gaily, indicating the bowl she carried in her arms. "You shall be satisfied with your board while you remain with me!"

Gildaen watched her arrange what she had picked for him. There was watercress, pearled with dew, and also young radishes and scallions, for which he had developed an interest in the palace kitchens, although as a cat he had not bothered to sample them.

"I've been wondering, Evonna, who has taken care of your garden while you were gone?" he asked as he paused between bites.

"Haven't you guessed?" she asked, surprised. "The birds are wonderful gardeners, Gildaen; I showed them long ago how to help me. They are the most meticulous weeders you can imagine, and they take care that no insect or worm robs me of the harvest. Last fall they gathered the seeds, and early in the spring they sowed them. Thanks to them, you are enjoying your fresh greens."

"There's no magic in your garden then?" he asked, a little disappointed.

"Perhaps a touch," she admitted. "But a lot of the magic is hard work, good earth, and sunshine!"

After their sunlit breakfast, they walked out together into the freshness of the morning. Gildaen could think of nothing to say.

"You are waiting, Gildaen?" she asked softly.

He merely nodded in reply. His throat felt dry, and he thought he would have trouble speaking.

"We will leave for the fortress at once. I have spent the night reading and thinking, and I see that you must take part in two more changes of form before our task is completed." She sat down on a garden bench beside a raised bed of blue and gold iris. "I planned first to visit Grimald's fortress pretending we were merchants wishing to buy herbs and potions. But the ride would take us too long a time. The fortress sits on the brow of a cliff, and the countryside around it is pocked with deep vales. Those who come must take this toilsome way, and they can be observed as they approach. When they are halfway up the last ascent, riders of Grimald go out to meet them and escort them the rest of the way. They are carefully guarded while they are within the fortress, and they are led out still under guard. That will not help us at all. I wish our entry there to be secret."

Gildaen nodded his agreement.

"Therefore, we will fly there. Do you remember that Fara once suggested I change us to birds? Now I can do so without fear that I will turn you into something else by mistake!"

Even as she spoke, Gildaen felt himself changing. His ears rang and his eyesight blurred for a few seconds. His nose felt quite odd. Then he was balancing on two claws instead of four paws. There were two heavy weights at his sides that he discovered were wings.

Before him stood one of the ancient enemies of his kind, with hooked beak and savage talons. The fierce eyes seemed to regard him coldly. He would have liked to run from that gaze, but he knew he would topple over. Then he realized that it was the Lady of Mallyn who faced him.

"You're a hawk!" he cried.

"As you are, Gildaen," she answered. "We must fly speedily today. No one will hinder us in these shapes. Come—see if you can fly!" She spread her wings and swept into the air.

Gildaen imitated her movements, and when he, too, had flapped the unfamiliar wings a few times, he felt himself leaving the ground. Birds from the hedges flew around him, calling instructions, not in the least afraid of him. Marveling at the ease of his flight, Gildaen rose higher and higher, leaving the songbirds behind.

"Farewell!" they called to him. "A safe flight!" chorused the doves, who settled back in a flurry of white to the cottage. He flew higher still until the cottage and the grove and gardens were specks of white, green, and a mass of bright colors, although his sight was so keen that he could easily discern the birds in the treetops. He was distressed to notice how easily a small creature such as a rabbit could be distinguished from this great height. He vowed to be more careful in open country in the future —"If there is a future for me!" he thought—and to keep one eye on the sky. As he gazed, he forgot to work at flying. A gust of wind caught him by surprise, and he turned over in midair, tumbling until he could hardly tell up from down and the breath was jolted from his body. As he turned beak over tail again, Evonna came up beside him.

"Your right wing," she urged. "Use your right wing to straighten out!"

He tried to do as she said and almost at once felt himself right side up.

"Now both wings, but easily, gently, Gildaen!"

With hardly an effort he found that he could glide and soar, changing his course by only a small movement of his marvelous wings.

"This is different from what I expected!" he called out to Evonna, who was flying close by. "I like it!"

"Of course!" she said. "But we have little time to amuse ourselves. A few more moments and we must be on our way."

Gildaen flew silently, wheeling over the witch's grove, getting the feel of the air currents, catching the trick of adjusting his wings to keep his balance as the wind changed.

Evonna had been observing him, and now she wheeled to the north, while he made haste to follow. He looked back quickly and caught one last glimpse of the cottage roof. The rolling meadows and plains they had crossed the day before were a sea of great smooth billows. The wind moved over vale and hill like a slow tide, ruffling the grasses. To the south, the king's forest was a solid mass of dark green. Away in the north he could make out a line of grayish brown that stretched across the horizon, and he knew that this was the mountainous land they

were seeking. Among those cliffs lay the fortress of the
Lord of the Bower.

They flew on silently for one hour and then another.
Gildaen found he needed to expend little energy, for the
wind was behind them and he could glide whenever he
chose. At noon with the sun directly overhead, he saw
their shadows cast on the land beneath them, two dark
shapes moving steadily northward. He saw small animals
of the field scurry for cover as those shadows passed over
them. He knew that they would breathe easier only when
they had passed. His thoughts were confusing. He was
one of those who had suffered constant fear of the strong,
hungry seekers of prey, and he understood the terror of
his kind. Yet now he knew something of the moods and
feelings of the hunters. He could never think of them
again with the same loathing and horror. "It doesn't seem
fair," he thought, "that cat and mouse can't change places,
even once, or that hawk and rabbit can't see things from
the other's point of view. But best of all would be a world
where one didn't have to eat or be eaten!"

"You are thinking hard thoughts, Gildaen," said Evonna,
flying a little closer.

"I was wishing that no creature needed to know fear,"
he said.

"A good wish," she said, "but not likely to come true."

"Is there no way?" he insisted.

She did not reply at once. Gildaen had almost given up
expecting her to speak when she answered. "Thinking has
never helped me find a way. Not one of the many books
you saw on my shelves has told me of a solution. Only
when I am with others, needing them, depending on them,
do I feel there is a possibility, a hard way. Do you know
what I mean?"

"I think so. When I first trusted you and asked to come with you, I felt it. I had to leave my own fear behind to help you and share your search."

"Yes, I know. Maybe that is one of the reasons I allowed you to come, my brash friend."

"When I became a cat, I saw life as a cat would, but I know that no cat will ever have a rabbit's outlook on the world."

"That is so. Each creature is shut in its own nature, unable to be other than what it is. You are fortunate to know what it is to be yourself—and more! Perhaps it is your fate to be a teacher of others."

Gildaen considered this comment. He had never thought of himself as having any knowledge. His travels had taught him much, had opened his eyes to the world.

He noticed that they had come close to the first line of hills. A few isolated dwellings were scattered below them, the property of the men who raised the horses that grazed and roamed on the wide grasslands.

The first highlands were green and fertile. Two roads from the south and east joined and ran through them. A party of travelers was making its way north along this road as it ascended. They broke their flight to circle above these men. His keen sight enabled Gildaen to see the clothing and even the upturned faces of the riders who were gazing at them. They were dressed in colorful silks and jeweled brocades, their hair covered with elaborate turbans. Gildaen took an immediate dislike to these travelers, who were now pointing upward and talking excitedly.

"They are merchants who have crossed the sea to trade with the Lord of the Bower," said Evonna.

"We must be close, then," Gildaen replied.

One of the men fitted an arrow to his elaborately carved

bow and aimed at Gildaen. The arrow fell far short, and
the two hawks sailed up and continued their northward
course.

Beyond the first highlands were others, no longer green,
but a bleak and bony wilderness where only a few trees
kept a tenacious hold on life. It was here, on a forbidding
height, that Gildaen saw the fortress. The road wound its
way through the stony wilds, between barren peaks, up a
tortuous ascent to the drawbridge, and there it ceased. The
fortress was inaccessible from any other approach, its sides
protected by the drop-away of the cliff.

Gildaen dreaded the thought of approaching that grim
hulk. He could scarcely believe that anything could be
grown within those forbidding walls, yet Evonna had assured him that the garden bloomed the entire year. As
they passed above the walls, they climbed higher. To the
eye of any who might be looking up, they appeared to be
gliding lazily, two hawks in mid-journey. In reality, they
were taking in as much of the view as they could. Gildaen
saw that after a traveler had crossed the drawbridge, he
would be forced to take a high-walled path leading directly
to the fortress, where armed guards would take his mount
to the stables. Thus, he would have no opportunity to see
the mysterious garden whose essences he had come to buy.
The fortress had no windows, only long slits in the stone
that served as meager inlets for light and air. Two watchtowers flanked it, commanding a view in every direction.
From these watchtowers guards could see approaching
travelers and give the signal to send out the escorting
riders.

Gildaen allowed himself the most time to look into
the garden, which to his amazement was as lush with
growth as if the season had been high summer. He could

discern trellises and arbors weighed down with heavy vines
in full bloom, and beds of brilliant-colored flowers. In the
center of the garden, as Evonna had explained, was the
bower, within which a jeweled fountain played, sending
up jets of water that sparkled in the sunlight. From the air
it appeared to be a place of glorious natural beauty. Gildaen longed to fly down and perch in one of the numerous
fruit trees. He could readily understand why Evonna had
yielded to that impulse. For the first time he acknowledged
the mastery of the Lord of the Bower. His senses told him
that he was looking at a paradise, but luckily for him, he
knew better.

"We should not attract undue attention," said Evonna.

He was dismayed at the thought that there might be
archers in the towers, undoubtedly with better aim than
the travelers on the road, men who would deem it good
sport to down two hawks on a slow afternoon. They flew
past the fortress, then turned, keeping low, seeking a con-
venient landing spot. There were a few stunted pines,
sinking stubborn roots into the unkind rocky ground.
One of these had been struck by lightning and split almost
in two. There were only a few remaining needles on this
blasted tree, and since no likelier place was in evidence,
they found uncomfortable perches in it.

"Only a vulture would be happy in such a roost,"
Evonna said, "but beggars cannot be choosers, and since
we come not even as beggars but as thieves, we must be
content."

Now that they were within a few wing flaps of their
objective, Gildaen's brain felt dry as dust. He could not
think of anything beyond holding onto his perch.

"You must go in soon, Gildaen," Evonna said, simply
and with finality.

Gildaen was struck by the fact that she had said "you" and not "we." He had not imagined that she would thrust the errand on him alone. How could he manage successfully without her guidance?

She said gently, "We dare not go together. If I should lose my memory again, I would be powerless to help either one of us. If you are in danger, I will risk it, of course, no matter what the price. For if you should fail, Gildaen"— and here she paused—"I must try my luck." Then the eyes softened. "But I do not expect that you will fail."

A notion of what failure might mean crossed his mind. Imprisonment in the fortress. Torture. A miserable end, alone and among enemies. Or, at the least, forgetfulness such as the Lady of Mallyn had suffered, leaving him to wander witlessly in the garden. With great clarity he recalled the sweet spring days in the Lower Wood and the steady contentment of watching the year move toward summer. He thought, too, of Hickory in his cell, and of the young king who might meet his end on the morrow if the Lord of the Bower had his way. He nodded his head miserably. Together they watched the golden afternoon disappear into the west, over the mountains. Evonna sat with closed eyes. Gildaen wondered if she was asleep, so still she was.

The fair evening light seemed to grow hard as it fell on the stone battlements of the fortress and the grim slopes surrounding it. When the sun was barely visible over the tallest mountains, Evonna opened her eyes. There was sadness in them as she looked at him, and Gildaen thought he detected something else there, too. Could it be admiration? His heart lifted at the thought.

"You will not forget, Gildaen," she said, as if she were continuing a conversation, "that for a creature to taste of any plant in that garden is to invite death, an agonizing death. I noticed that the monkshood was particularly beautiful as we flew over the garden, and so was the meadow saffron, but a few nibbles would mean death. The berries of the nightshade are tempting, and they are, in truth, sweet, but just as deadly. I have no fear that you would want to sample the henbane; it smells as odious as it looks."

"Do you imagine I would eat anything in *there?*" Gildaen asked, amazed.

"You don't think so now," she replied. "Wait until you encounter these plants and you may understand why I take the trouble to remind you! But your disguise should protect you in case you lose your head and disobey me anyway." She left her perch and flew to the foot of the sheer stone wall that protected the fortress on every side. Gildaen alighted beside her, and she whispered, "I shall change you into one who should not need to fear poison."

She stared at him, and he experienced grievous pain; the breath was being crushed from him; he was being squeezed in an unyielding vise. His legs disappeared, as did his wings. This transformation was so much worse than any of the others he had undergone that Gildaen hardly knew if he were alive or dead. What could Grimald's men do to him that was any worse than this, he thought? He lay exhausted among the rocks on the dry earth. Slowly the spasms of pain receded and were gone. He was left with a long string of a body that he did not know how to move.

"I am sorry the change was painful, Gildaen," Evonna whispered. "You had to be made quite different. It will be much easier when I arrange you back the way you ought to be. Listen carefully now. You have the entire night to search. The more I reflect, the more certain I am that the talisman is not in the fortress, but in the bower itself, and it is there that I would have you search. Take your time, Gildaen, and when you find the talisman, try to bring it back with you. I shall be waiting for you at sunrise, here, outside the walls."

"What do I look like?" he asked, a little fearful of knowing.

"You are bright green, the color of grass in a well-tended garden. Your eyes are like yellow jewels, and you are as poisonous as you are handsome. I have given you the form of a snake, Gildaen, a viper whose sting is death. No one who sees you will want to have anything to do with you!"

He grasped the logic of the disguise. It would make him safe in the garden, a poisoner among poisons.

"Try to move your body from side to side," coaxed Evonna. "Moving straight ahead won't work; you must slither first to one side and then to the other in order to go forward."

Gildaen tried to obey these instructions. At last he managed to control his jerky motions and found that Evonna was right. In order to go in the direction he wanted, he had to weave to the left and right of that direction. Once he had grasped this principle, he was able to slide without difficulty, avoiding the broken rocks that had hurt him when he attempted to move across them. He quickly acquired agility and even some speed.

The mountains were a somber gray. Twilight was giving way to night. Gildaen undulated to the foundation of the fortress walls, seeking an entrance, but the wall was solid. He slid among broken rock and boulders, searching in vain until he spied a chink near the corner of the western wall. He lifted his head and saw Evonna watching him.

"Good hunting!" she called, so softly that he wondered if he had heard anything at all. He slipped into the chink and disappeared from her view.

The Lady of Mallyn's thoughts ran back to her first meeting with the rabbit who had trembled on the ground before her. How frightened he had been, too frightened even to speak! She raised her head and listened, but heard only remote noises from the fortress, the horses in their stables, guards laughing together, and a wind from the mountains moving across the slopes. She flew to her perch in the lightning-blasted pine. It would be a long night.

INTO THE BOWER

WHEN GILDAEN SLID HIS NEW BODY THROUGH the crack, he had no idea what to expect on the other side. He knew that he would come out within the garden itself, but he was not sure what he would find there. He listened tensely for the sound of guards patrolling the grounds until he remembered that he should be able to elude any guard and that any guard would want to escape him. He emerged among thick thorn bushes growing along the wall. The Lord of the Bower had designed his plantings cleverly. Anyone able to scale the wall would have to jump into a waiting bed of spikes. The thorns were long and sharp. No man would survive such a landing. He glided easily through the bushes, close to the ground, grateful again to the Lady of Mallyn for giving him a shape so well suited to his needs.

He came out of the thorns into the shadow of fruit trees. These were planted in neat double rows that followed the line of the wall. Glancing upward, he saw that each tree bore many different kinds of fruit grafted upon the parent tree. Some were already temptingly ripe, while others were only beginning to mature. He noticed that the air was much warmer than it had been outside the walls. Though it was a cool April night in the hills, the balminess of summer was in the air here, making him feel sluggish. He could easily imagine Evonna falling asleep in the branches of one of these trees. He heard a splashing not too far away, and he recalled the fountain he had seen from the air. He determined to make his way to this central part of the garden, into the bower itself, as quickly as possible. He slipped from under the fruit trees across one of the paths that led maze-like deeper and deeper into the heart of the garden. The path was soft on his belly, strewn with fine-grained white sand that shone dimly in the light of the newly risen moon. On the other side of the path were raised beds of flowers, bordered by what looked like a common vegetable. This border plant had the fringed leaves common to carrots and parsnips. Gildaen recognized it as the deadly hemlock. His cousin Rafe had died suddenly after nibbling just a little from such a plant growing wild in the meadow.

Many of the blossoms were closed to the night air, but others appeared to be opening as the moon rose higher. White roses, larger and heavier than any Gildaen had seen before, occupied the entirety of one of these raised beds. He paused as he came alongside them, for their perfume was such that he could not resist tarrying to smell it. He thought that he would never forget their haunting fragrance, sweet and overpowering. He was tempted to stay here beside them, even to creep into the bed and lie there, breathing in their scent until the morning came. He sighed and roused himself from the drugging effect of the flowers. "A place of many dangers!" he thought, as he hastened to leave them behind.

He crossed the path twice more as it wove inward toward the center, until he came to the circular arbor that marked the entry to the bower itself. This arbor was of graceful latticework, covered over with flowering vines whose fragrance was even more powerful but less appealing to Gildaen than that of the roses had been. Woven in among these vines was ivy, an artificial ivy fashioned of fine golden wires and gilded leaves, gleaming in the moonlight. Marble benches were placed at intervals in this arbor, as were statues cleverly carved in various kinds of marble. So lifelike were these that Gildaen came to a sudden halt when he saw the first of them, a great fanged beast with glaring eyes that fixed him with their brilliance. After a few endless-seeming minutes, Gildaen came to the realization that the beast, crouched for a spring, was really a statue with precious jewels for eyes. He moved ahead, past more strange animals of stone, each caught in the pose of rearing to strike, the jeweled eyes glittering with a passion for death that was altogether too realistic for Gildaen. He followed the arbor full circle, back to the place where he had entered it. He decided to go directly into the center of the bower through one of the four openings in the latticework. The greensward tickled him pleasantly as he slithered into the well-tended circle. There were circular herb beds next to the arbor, following its curvature. At the very middle of the bower was the fountain whose musical jets and splashes had been growing steadily louder.

The base of this fountain was formed from the whitest of alabaster. A circular basin received the water from a smaller basin above it, made of a blood-red porphyry. A statue rose from this second basin in the form of a stone chalice, an elaborate footed cup, covered with gold filigree and studded with jewels of every color. From the chalice came the jets of clear water that tumbled from one basin to another. At the foot of this impressive fountain was a thick mass of vine, sinuous, thick, fleshy, whose tendrils reached out to every part of the fountain from the base to the foot of the gilded chalice.

"Ugly!" thought Gildaen, repulsed by this uncomely plant in a garden of botanical marvels.

He lifted himself as well as he could to survey the bower. "Where can the talisman be?" he wondered. As he glided past the fountain, he felt an odd revulsion for which he could not account. He made his way to a table and chair that stood near the herbs on the opposite side of the glade. Both table and chair were heavily ornamented with vines and flowers wrought in gilt. There was something on the table, but Gildaen could not make out what it was. He glanced around cautiously once more, but since there was nothing to be seen or heard save the lulling sound of the water in the fountain, he slithered up the table leg and onto the top. He was delighted to see two objects on the table. He dared to hope that one of them might give him a clue to the whereabouts of the talisman. One proved to be a pair of silver shears, and the other a small book. The shears had been used as a weight to hold the book open at a certain page. The book was very old, and the writing was blurred and faint with age. The

Lord of the Bower had been reading this very page before
his last visit to the court. "But that was long ago," he
thought. "And Grimald is clearly a man who prizes
secrecy, a man who trusts no one. Why would he leave
his book open for any casual eye to see?" He began to
wonder, too, why he had encountered no living creature
in all of the garden, and he dearly wished that Evonna
had taught him to read. He consoled himself with the
thought that this book was probably written in a language
only Grimald could decipher. He tried to understand the
reason for the presence of the shears, and decided they
were probably there so that Grimald could snip a flower
or an herb at his will. But again the question came to
mind: Why did he leave these possessions in full view of
any of his men who might come here? There was a mystery
in that question which he could not penetrate. He no
longer suspected that either of these objects would afford
him a clue. He draped himself across the open page. From
the tabletop he had a good view of the entire bower, and
he could not forbear admiring the scene—the delicate
latticework of the arbor with the golden ivy worked among
the real vines, the velvet grass pearled with dew, the
fountain sending up crystal jets of water that sparkled in
the full light of the moon, which was shining just overhead.

As he looked with unwilling respect at the Lord of the
Bower's handiwork, he was suddenly aware that the vine
around the fountain had moved. A low sound unlike anything Gildaen had ever heard was coming from it while
it lifted its tendrils as if to bathe them in the moonlight.
It writhed, twining and untwining, a serpent of greenery
performing a kind of dreadful dance. Its blossoms began
to open with a hideous popping sound.

There was the squeak of a gate opening and shutting, and then the sound of hurrying footsteps. A guard appeared presently at one of the entrances to the arbor, looking none too happy to be there. He carried a large cage in each hand, filled with rats collected from the fortress.

"Here, you blasted vegetable, take 'em!" he muttered fearfully as he crossed the grass. He stopped a good ten feet from the fountain, swung open the doors of both cages, then turned on his heel and ran, never pausing until the gate into the garden was clanged shut again.

The rats hesitated in their cages, until one bolder than the rest ran out to seek his freedom. He covered only a short distance before the vine sent out a sinuous shoot that caught him, lifted him to one of the newly opened blossoms, and dropped him within it. Quick as thought the blossom closed fast on him. The same fate came to each of the fleeing rats, scurry though they might and struggle though they tried. The vine waited until the last rat had almost succeeded in reaching the shelter of the arbor before snaring him neatly around the middle.

"Almost as if the thing were toying with him!" thought Gildaen, overcome with disgust. The feeding had been a horrible sight, over in a few minutes. The blossoms were shut tight again, and the vine was humming with satisfaction. Soon the tendrils ceased their writhing and were still, innocently draped about the fountain.

Gildaen knew now why the Lord of the Bower left his possessions so carelessly in sight and why he expected to find them untouched when he returned. He had left a watchman here, a guard who was rightly feared and loathed. The vine was a meat eater and probably not particular about what that meat was! He remembered his revulsion when he had passed the fountain. Why had the vine not snared him, he wondered? Perhaps it was not yet fully awake, or perhaps, he calculated, the poison in his being had repelled it. He was fully awake to the meaning of the vine's presence. The Lord of the Bower employed it as a guard, which meant that there was something precious here which needed protection, something to do with the fountain. "Evonna was right," he thought, "the talisman is somewhere here." But where? The shears and the book were only carelessly tended belongings of Grimald's.

He looked down at the neatly clipped grass. Could the talisman be buried near the fountain? If so, his errand was a hopeless one. There was no way in which he could dig up the glade before morning. But he recalled that Evonna had said the talisman was probably in plain sight. She had been unerring in her guesses thus far, and she was sure to be right in this as well. He must look as she would look, trying to understand where the Lord of the Bower would find it amusing to keep his talisman. He glanced around the bower again, and the truth hit him like a thunderbolt: the chalice! He studied the glittering cup, studded with every variety of gem. There were emeralds, rubies, sapphires, diamonds. One stone, he noticed, only one, was a dull black. In an instant the picture came to him of Grimald's cloak clasp, as he had seen it at the king's palace, set with an identical stone. This was its twin! This must be the talisman, he thought excitedly; perhaps both stones were necessary to Grimald! He could have shouted for glee as he saw how cleverly the Lord of the Bower had thought to hide his treasure in the open. It was displayed so that he might see it and take pleasure in his cunning whenever he came to the bower. He had set a deadly guardian on the fountain, rejoicing in his wit and in his deadly sentry.

Gildaen was faced with a dilemma. How could he secure the jewel and yet escape the vine? His time was growing short. He gave the vine his complete attention: except for the motion of the breeze ruffling a tendril here and there, he saw no trace of movement in the thing. To an unwary eye, it would appear like any other plant, unusual only for its size and ugliness. He must take the chance that the vine was dull with feeding, ready to slumber through the coming day. So great was his disgust for it that he could not imagine performing his task. He struggled with his emotions. "I must do it," he thought. "Today is the third day. If I wait for Evonna to help me, it may be too late for the king and Hickory." He forced himself to move to the table's edge and drop soundlessly into the grass.

He made his way to the base of the fountain and hesitated. He would have to cross the vine itself to reach the basin. Worse still, there was no way to go from the larger basin to the smaller and from there to the chalice without using the vine as a bridge! He felt sick at the idea of touching it. But he saw that there was no other way. The pale gray light in the east was a warning that the night would soon be over.

With every ounce of his will, he compelled himself to glide onto the vine. Instead of the clammy surface he had persuaded himself he would feel, the vine was warm, pulsing slowly, and it was covered with fine fuzzy hairs. He swallowed and moved on more rapidly, climbing up to the first basin, and onward to the second. After what seemed to Gildaen to be an eternity, he reached the level of the chalice itself.

He felt the throbbing increase in tempo, as if the

creature were rousing. The low humming began again, and the vine started to twitch. The watchman was waking up, and woe to the intruder! He slid hurriedly onto the gilded surface of the chalice itself, grateful to leave the vine. He searched frantically for the black jewel. The vine was writhing now. If it had been an animal, Gildaen would have said that it was bellowing. He heard it demand in a speech unlike any other, "Who are you? Who dares trespass here!"

A tendril sought him. His tongue flicked out, and the tendril fell back, limp. At least he had the ability to do the vine some harm, he thought. He glided past an emerald, a ruby, an amethyst—and then he saw it, the black stone. But even as he came to it, his hopes were dashed. Like gems in a ring, the stones were held out from the side of the chalice on prongs of gold. He had no way to pry it loose!

The tendrils were all around him. He poisoned a few, and the others withdrew momentarily as the vine howled with fury and baffled rage.

Gildaen knew, though, that he was trapped. He could not fight the vine indefinitely. He would be strangled in the end. In his desperation an idea came to him. At once he swung himself onto the black jewel and coiled his body tightly around it. An instant later the vine caught him in two tendrils, twin nooses that pulled ever tighter. He could not breathe. He was being crushed, a small serpent strangled by a greater. With his last strength he held on to the jewel. There was a sharp metallic crack as the gold prongs anchoring the gem gave way and broke off. Gildaen, still holding on to the stone, felt himself raised on high. Dully, he wondered if the vine would try to eat him. Then there was a hideous scream that pierced his brain, a shuddering sigh, and Gildaen felt himself falling through the air.

He was flung onto the grass, gasping for breath. The first light of a clear morning was in the sky. Before his up-turned eyes he saw the vine fling its tendrils wildly in every direction, but even as he watched, it withered, dying, until there was only a tangled mass of pulpy rubbish surrounding the fountain. A chill was in the air, the chill of a spring morning. The balmy summer heat was gone. The fragrant vines in the arbor were withering too, as if a sudden frost had laid them waste.

The fountain had abruptly stopped playing, and in all the garden no sound was to be heard. Gildaen was dazed. His body ached from the bruising pressure of the vine. Weakly he uncurled himself from the black jewel, a pain-ful maneuver. He wished that he could close his eyes and sleep.

A raucous caw sounded above him, and he opened his weary eyes to see the sky filled with circling black birds.

"The blasted garden's gone to ruination!" cawed one of their number, hovering over the arbor.

"Done for!" shouted another. "The guardian's dead!"

At this, there were shouts of jubilation, and at least half a dozen crows flew down and alighted on the vine, pecking at it and rending it. Others alighted on the chalice and eagerly tried to pry out the brilliant jewels.

A voice Gildaen recognized said, "I'll take that, thank you!" and the leader of the flock swooped down and picked up the black stone in one claw. Gildaen remem-bered the name that went with that voice—it was Chough. How he came to be here, Gildaen did not care, but he would have given anything to have prevented the theft of the talisman he had risked his life for.

"Let's finish off the snake," cawed a crow who had been tearing at the vine.

"Right-o!" cried another, and they circled over Gildaen, hurling insults at him and shrieking with laughter at his plight. He remembered his dream of two nights before and wished numbly that this, too, were a dream. He made up his mind that he would poison as many of the outlaws as he could before they finished him.

There was confusion in the sky, and the birds turned their attention from him. Black feathers were falling like rain around him. A large hawk was making short work of the crows, and he looked up in time to see the hawk sink its talons into Chough. The black stone came hurtling from the sky back into the clearing. A screech of fear and pain rang out as the hawk shook the crow like a limp rag and tossed him into the air. The rest of the outlaw flock was undecided about what to do. There were cries of "Let's go for the hawk!" but most were cawing their alarm and scattering for safety.

"Cowards and scoundrels as ever!" came the clear sound of Evonna's voice. "Creep away to do mischief in solitary secrecy!" Then the birds were gone, and tiny black shapes fell from the air.

Evonna landed close to Gildaen. "They are scorpions now," she said, the anger gone from her voice. "Perhaps they will sting their master when he returns here."

She found the black jewel where it had fallen and picked it up in her beak. When she returned to Gildaen, she took him up with the greatest care in both talons, rising into the sky with her double burden. Gildaen was too weak and weary to think of the future.

Below them lay the garden of the mighty Grimald. The trees were barren of leaf and fruit. The flowers and herbs

were withered and ruined. In that barren spot there was
no trace of green. Men were gazing down on it from the
watchtower, and guards were running toward the garden.
"Too late," Gildaen thought. Evonna rose higher and
veered southward. Gildaen could see only a blur of sunlight and feel the wind on his tormented body. Of that
journey he remembered nothing more.

WHICH IS HOME?

 N A WARM MORNING IN EARLY MAY, ALMOST two weeks after his rescue from the bower, Gildaen was able to get out of his basket. He wobbled when he walked, and his bones ached when he moved suddenly. It was too much of an effort for him to hold his ears up, so they flopped around his face. Even his whiskers drooped.

"You are better today," said Evonna, smiling at him as he slowly ate his breakfast.

"Yes," he agreed, "I think I must be."

Of the previous days he recalled little, but he knew that he had seen Fara's face often, and he was sure he had glimpsed Hickory staring anxiously down at him on more than one occasion.

"Well," she asked, "have you no questions you wish to have answered?"

"I thought you would tell me everything when I was ready to hear it," he replied meekly.

"*Now* you worry me, Gildaen!" she said with a laugh. "Since when have you waited to be told what you wished to know?"

"I am too sore to talk much," he answered truthfully.

"Say nothing, then, and listen, for I must talk to you before the others return. Fara's mother has sent for her. She wants Fara to come home, and as soon as possible. Fara will ask you to live with her, but Hickory is just as eager that you remain here in the palace with him."

"Wait, please," Gildaen said. "Is Hickory free? Did I only dream that he was here, watching over me?"

"He was released the morning you took the talisman from the chalice. Because of your success, our friend Grimald lost his chance to poison the king. He and his henchmen rode off at top speed in the direction of his fortress."

"But why didn't he go through with his plan? I still don't understand," Gildaen said.

"When the black stone was wrested from the chalice, it was no longer his but yours, Gildaen. The enchantments he had made with it were set at naught. The king's eyes were opened to Grimald's true nature. After that, he would never have allowed Grimald or his imposter physician to approach him. And why do you imagine you escaped from the vine? Only because it was destroyed along with the rest of the garden when you gained the talisman."

Gildaen shivered. His body would long bear bruises inflicted by the vine. At length he said, "I was sure I was done for. First the vine and then the crows!"

"I suppose Chough must have led his cutthroats back to Grimald after I transformed them. He probably thought that Grimald had the magic to undo the change, but I doubt the Lord of the Bower thought it more than a good joke! They were the first to try to gain advantage from his downfall, but I wager they'll not be the last. The Lord of the Bower has made many enemies!" she said cheerfully.

"What will he do now, do you think?" asked Gildaen. He was certain that such a man would not rest content with his present lot.

"There is nothing he can do. I suspect he will have to deal with a mutiny at the fortress. Probably he means to shut himself up until he can find a way to nurture his garden and his broken spells. But he shall have to manage without his talisman."

"Do you have it?" he asked, curious. He would have been glad of the chance to examine the stone more closely.

"Not here," she said. "It is safe, I promise you. *He* shall never regain it."

The door was quietly opened by Fara. Hickory came in behind her, dressed in hunting garb, the red and gold royal emblem embroidered at the collar. "At last you're awake, Gildaen!" said Fara. "I have so much to tell you! Evonna will scold me if I say only half I wish to. She's been a jealous nurse, Gildaen. There's little she would let any but herself do for you."

"I am glad to see you both!" Gildaen replied, giddy with joy at the sight of his friends, while they in turn looked relieved and happy.

Hickory sat down on the floor beside Gildaen.

"I recollect you do not like to have to crane your neck to look up at me, Gildaen," he said, reminding him of their conversation in the forest. Then his face became serious as he gazed at the rabbit. "You are too scrawny by half for the stewpot," he said.

"But you look wonderful, Hickory," said Gildaen, and indeed it was true. Hickory's eyes had a light in them none of them had seen there before. His bearing, the way he held his head, the quality of his voice, all bespoke his happiness at being again where he belonged.

"I have you to thank for it, Gildaen, if you see me looking well. My young master, the king, is himself, just as he was before Grimald came. I cannot repay this favor, no matter how long I live, but I would be glad to try. Will you stay here with me, Gildaen? I will keep you safe and see you lack nothing, I promise!" he said solemnly. This was a long speech for Hickory, and having made it, he sat back, awaiting an answer.

"Don't make up your mind yet, Gildaen," pleaded Fara. "I want you to come to us! Mother said in her message I might ask you. You know what good times we had together when you stayed with us!"

The breeze wafted in the perfume of roses from the courtyard. Gildaen imagined what it would be like to live in the palace every day, to be confined indoors unless Hickory accompanied him, to grow as fat and lazy as Rustrim. He had a vivid picture of what would happen to him should he meet one of the palace cats in his true shape! As for Fara's invitation, he wondered how it would be to live in Farmer Liddle's house. He had been happy with Fara and her mother on their farm, but to depend on Farmer Liddle's good graces was not much to his liking. He did not wish to offend either of his friends.

Both were intent on making him happy, but he did not want to say yes to either.

Evonna had been watching him closely as he mulled over their offers, and now she came to his rescue. She said to him, "Gildaen, the summer is almost here. We know how happy you are in the wild. Do you want to return to your own home?"

He bowed his head. "I don't wish to seem ungrateful! I love each of you, yet—" He hesitated.

"Go on," urged Hickory.

"Yet I would like to go back to the Lower Wood! For now, I mean. For the summer. I have a longing to see my family and the familiar places again. But when the leaves turn, I shall think back on our adventures." He in his turn waited shyly.

Evonna seemed to understand exactly what he had in mind. "Will you spend the autumn and winter with me, Gildaen? Hickory will be less than a day's ride from my cottage, and I shall contrive it that Fara shall join us, too."

"Yes!" he cried, taking a shaky hop.

And so it was settled. A few days later Gildaen left the palace discreetly in his basket. The Walloons bade their visitors a long and affectionate farewell.

"Good-bye, little Fara. I expect you'll not miss me at all," said Walter Walloon, giving her a kiss. He turned to Evonna. "I'll never have such an assistant again," he mourned, shaking his head.

The wagon had been amply provisioned by the Walloons, and now Hickory, who was to ride a part of the way with them, brought up his own horse as well as Meg and Sall. A flurry of trumpets announced King Justin and Lord Royce. Evonna curtsied deeply and withdrew a few steps from her friends for a brief conversation with the king and his minister. The Walloons were too good-natured to stare, but they were plainly startled by her easy familiarity with royalty.

Lord Royce himself helped Fara and Evonna into the wagon. "We are forever in your debt, my lady," he said to her in a low voice, "and we await your return."

Good-byes were exchanged all around once more, the horses neighed impatiently, and the journey was begun. Hickory rode with them for the better part of the journey until they were only a day's ride from the farm. Then they said good-bye. Gildaen reminded himself that he would be seeing Hickory again before too long.

Gildaen watched until Hickory's tall figure was only a speck in the distance. The horses were eager, almost frolicksome. They knew this road, and they decided they must be heading for home. Evonna had to calm them often to keep them at a steady pace. They reached the farm at twilight, and their welcome was as joyful as their departure had been bleak. Millicent Liddle hugged them each in turn and could not get enough of gazing at Fara. "You've grown," she said, "and what a pretty gown you have on! My sister has been good to you!" and she hugged her daughter again.

They had a happy evening together, feasting on the hearty supper set before them. Though the good farmer was as kind a host as one could wish for, Gildaen thought he saw a look of relief in his eyes when Evonna told him that she and Gildaen would depart on the morrow. He was too honest a man to pretend that magic and talking rabbits suited him. They told some of their adventures, but not all, leaving out what they thought their listeners would find hardest to believe. Fara's mother was most interested in news of her relatives and in the fashion of dress in the palace, whereas her husband questioned Evonna closely about the stables. He was clearly delighted to see his best team of horses safely home again, shaking his head at the luck of it.

Gildaen took the opportunity to have a lengthy chat with Chanticleer late that night. The rooster steadfastly refused to believe any of Gildaen's tales, but he was very polite, remarking that it was the duty of travelers to bring back unusual stories to entertain their friends. Then he proceeded to give Gildaen a detailed account of their moving day with its many difficulties, until he noticed that Gildaen had fallen asleep halfway through the narration.

In the morning Gildaen learned that Evonna had talked earnestly with Millicent Liddle about her daughter's future, and it had been agreed Fara should spend each fall and winter as the pupil of the Lady of Mallyn. "I can see," said Fara's mother, "that she's meant for something other than a farm life," but her voice was wistful.

Evonna left on foot, much to the distress of their host and hostess, but no insistence could change her mind. She carried Gildaen in his basket. "We have a pleasant walk ahead of us, the weather is fair, and I shall not need a horse after I leave Gildaen," she said with a twinkle in her eye.

"Good-bye, Evonna! Farewell, Gildaen!" Fara called after them. "Do not forget me till we meet again!"

The farm folk they saw in their fields gaped in surprise at the sight of a lone woman striding down the road at a brisk pace. The weather was what one would always like, if one could choose, bright and warm, with the suggestion of a breeze. Gildaen became more and more excited as they neared his home. He pointed out the landmarks as the farmland gave way to gentle wooded slopes. When they came to a grove of ancient cedars, he insisted he would be carried no longer and that he was well able to run. "Over the next hill you will see it!" he said, and his meaning was made clear when Evonna glimpsed the battlements of the ruined castle before her. A new season's growth of ivy was beginning to mantle the walls. Finally they drew near the splintered drawbridge and came to a halt, facing each other.

"Well, Gildaen, are you happy?" asked the Lady of Mallyn.

"Too happy for words!" he answered, sniffing the softly scented air. His fur was warm with sun, and there, in that familiar place, he could hardly believe that he had not dreamed his adventures.

"Until the fall, then!" she said. The figure in the brown dress shrunk and was transformed into the hawk who had taken him from the bower. She rose from the grass, almost brushing his back with her talons. A few swift wing-strokes took her high into the midday sky. Gildaen had to squint into the sun to find her, and soon she was lost to his sight. He glanced around, and there was the wicker basket in the grass where the Lady of Mallyn had left it. He would hide it and keep it safe.

AFTERWARDS

 HEN GILDAEN RETURNED TO THE LOWER WOOD, he found himself a hero to his brothers and sisters and his numerous relatives. Since the young ones especially clamored to hear his adventures over and over, it became a favorite pastime with him to describe his entry into the bower and his battle with the vine. The elders sometimes grumbled that the tall tales would addle the children's brains and send them out seeking mad escapades, but they need not have feared; no other rabbit showed the least desire to imitate Gildaen.

The Lady of Mallyn came for him in the fall. He left with a light heart, promising to return in the spring. They fetched Fara from the Liddle farm, and this time they journeyed in a light, well-sprung coach drawn by two matched bays that King Justin insisted the Lady of Mallyn use for conveying her charges. Gildaen's pleasure was complete when he heard that Hickory planned to ride over to visit them as often as he could.

Days in the grove were filled with work in the gardens, and the evenings in the cottage were over too soon, there in the candlelight and the fireglow. True to her word, the Lady of Mallyn taught Gildaen as well as Fara the names and uses of plants. She showed them how to dry herbs and distill essences, to make decoctions and prepare electuaries. She read to them from her books, instructing both in the secrets of healing.

Gildaen's arrival in the Lower Wood each spring became an eagerly awaited event. He had new tales to tell and brought with him seeds that grew into tasty summer fare. At first he held a hedge infirmary every other morning, and then every morning, for as his fame spread, many made their way to him, even beasts of prey. Foxes, weasels, hawks, and owls went so far as to instruct their young to avoid hunting in his neighborhood, an order that made Gildaen's hill a haven for rabbits and other small animals.

It became common knowledge for miles around that a rabbit physician lived in the Lower Wood. Since he was kind and sympathetic as well as skillful and learned, he was greatly respected. And because he became neither pompous nor conceited, he was loved as well.